HIDDEN

David Berardelli

HIDDEN

GRAVESTONE PRESS

PART ONE

THE HUNTED

Chapter 1 - 6:30 P.M.

The silver Porsche 911R zipped west on I-70 at a comfortable speed of 75.

"You know that seat is totally adjustable, don'tcha?" Craig Sheffield gave her a quick glance.

"I know."

"Then why don't you—"

"I'm okay."

"You don't look okay. Actually, you look…well, uncomfortable."

"I'm *fine*."

He shrugged and turned back to his driving.

Bobbie Marsh sighed and told herself she wouldn't give him the satisfaction of being right. True, she *was* uncomfortable, and had been growing even more so since they left Wheeling. She sat ramrod-straight, her right side mashed against the leather contour of the passenger door. She stared straight ahead at the endless trail of taillights in front of them. Not once did she glance in his direction. But she didn't care *how* adjustable the seat was. She didn't *want* to be comfortable. If she was comfortable, she might be compliant, and she certainly didn't want that. Not with her boss once again calling all the shots.

She would have preferred spending the last hour of the work week at her cube, doing mindless busywork, than doing this. However, Craig had a way of getting what he wanted. And after working for him for the last six months, she knew full well how badly things could go when he didn't get his way. There would be extra work tossed onto her desk, emails flooding her mailbox, and several days when crucial jobs would mysteriously enter her queue five minutes before quitting time that would have to be resubmitted and rerun.

She saw no need to get worked up again. She'd do as he ordered and take this twenty-minute trip to check out his new real estate property, and she'd smile on cue and nod on cue. However, going by his past behavior, she could tell this was just another ruse to get her alone. As always, she told herself to be on her guard.

He glanced at her. "I can tell you really didn't want to come on this trip, Bobbie."

She thought it best not to say anything. She wasn't in the mood to argue. She wanted to get this done as quickly as possible. She couldn't wait to get back to the office so she could jump in her Camaro, drive back to her one-bedroom garden apartment and begin enjoying her weekend.

"As I told you before, it won't take long—no more than an hour, I expect. But I'm really excited about this property and would like your expert opinion. I consider you a valuable asset to the company, so I'd appreciate your input."

Bobbie still didn't reply. She kept her eyes straight ahead, at the approaching Ohio countryside.

She told herself to stay in control and let him do his thing. Putting up with his nonsense for another hour would be no different from putting up with it at the office. She was making good money at Sheffwares and saw no need to jeopardize her career just because he'd ruined her plans for the weekend. He'd shanghaied her several times before, so what was the big deal?

It *was* a big deal, of course, even though she'd almost convinced herself she could handle it. He'd been trying his level best to make her his mistress ever since she'd filled out her application at Sheffwares and sat in his office for her first interview. He'd been subtle about it in the beginning, but she recognized the signs right off. Luckily, she'd been offered much more than she'd expected. Otherwise, she would have turned him down cold. But at twenty-five, a girl had to start thinking of the big picture and warding off conniving wolves like Craig Sheffield became part of the process. Like it or not, the business world was run prominently by men.

"I'd like to turn the property into a golf course." He gave her a quick glance. "It'll cost a fortune to clear, of course, but I'm confident the return will more than make up for the initial outlay. The hills and creeks are perfect for it, and the woods behind it could provide a beautiful setting for a restaurant and bar. Once you have a look and tell me what you think, we'll head right back to the office."

Just as they passed the Bridgeport area, Craig took the next exit and went south. He drove the

Porsche onto a two-lane road, which abruptly turned into a narrow dirt road just a mile or so later. They came to a three-way stop. Craig turned right and went straight for about another mile, until the road grew even narrower and bumpier. Bobbie was about to ask where this place was when Craig suddenly slowed and turned off, where a break in the tree line showed evidence of a dirt path and a barbed wire fence that had deteriorated and collapsed over the years, becoming part of the thick brush. He drove up the winding forty-five-degree dirt drive, which seemed to go on forever, until they reached the top of the hill, where a large farmhouse stood, fortress-like, nestled among the trees.

To Bobbie, the property looked dismal, the setting sun peeking through the branches of the buckeyes, revealing an aged, tired-looking farmhouse with no sign of life anywhere near it.

Craig coaxed the sleek ride up the steep drive. He stopped in front of the big house, put the car in park, set the emergency brake and switched off the ignition.

"Well?" He grinned proudly, waving an arm. He gave her the impression that he'd single-handedly cleared the woods and built the house with his own two hands. "A honey of a place, eh?"

Bobbie glanced at her watch. 6:58. It would be dusk in half an hour. Unless he'd had the electricity switched over in his name, she wouldn't be able to see anything very shortly. She also hoped he didn't want her to trudge through the woods in the dark.

"Well? Your first impression?" He was waiting anxiously.

Reluctantly she peeled herself away from the door. She knew she'd definitely have to humor him. Craig was excited. It would be a crime to burst his bubble. But she had no intention of staying here any longer than it took to check out the property and tell him it was fine and dandy, and yes, he was a good boy for getting it at such a great price. Then she'd give her watch another not-so-subtle glance and tell him that she'd had enough fun and frolic for the afternoon, had seen all there was to see, and wanted to get back home.

She forced her attention back to the house. Its isolation, along with its darkened windows, missing shingles, peeling paint and look of total neglect, made her slightly nauseous. A shiver passed through her, and she sensed a strange darkness she didn't much care for. "It looks...haunted," she said softly.

Craig laughed. One of those snorty things which, like most everything he did, disgusted her. "That's just the outside," he said, patting her thigh. "Coat of paint'll do wonders. I intend to convert it to a Cracker Barrel-type place anyway—one that sells knickknacks and homemade jellies and honey."

She pulled away from him and hoped he wouldn't try that again.

Craig got out, closed the door, looked around for a moment and slowly scaled the steps.

Bobbie refocused and regarded the wooden porch, where thick, weathered pillars stood proudly, oblivious of the years that had gradually weakened them. She thought it just as eerie—and as desolate—as the house in *Psycho*. It didn't exactly look like the type of place you bought to convert into a warm, cozy store selling knickknacks and gifts. For a moment she wondered if there was a corpse sitting in a rocker in the basement.

"Coming in?" He'd turned and was gesturing.

With a tired sigh, she swung her slender, denim-clad legs out of the Porsche and pulled the strap of her black leather bag over her left shoulder. As she approached the house, she couldn't ignore the honest gloom settling around it as she gazed at it from just twenty feet away.

Was it gloom? Or something else?

Something about Craig?

Bobbie had always been forced to use her instincts with men. If she had strong feelings about someone, she went with those feelings and let nature take its course. If things worked out, fine; if not, she went on with her life.

In this case, something inside her constantly warned her against getting close to him. He was good-looking, well-dressed, and outgoing. And, from what she'd already seen, he was very popular with women. She knew he was married but also knew from painful experience that marriage meant nothing to wealthy men. She'd heard that Craig had been separated from his wife Colleen for some time. She'd also heard that they'd been seriously considering divorce, but Colleen's interest in Sheffwares would make things very difficult for everyone involved.

However, Bobbie had learned never to put much stock into office gossip—especially when it involved the boss's friends and drinking buddies.

Gripping the straps of her bag, she sniffed the sweet scents of the pines and the fresh autumnal grass. She approached the three cracked, weather-beaten logs serving as the front porch steps and scaled them slowly and cautiously, as if approaching an awaiting guillotine.

The house was quite warm inside. The living room had that distinctive musty smell a place has when it's been closed up, though Craig told her that the realtor had paid someone to come in recently and clean it up.

At least it was cozy...

She envisioned cold nights on the sofa, watching the flames crackling in the fireplace, wine glasses in warm hands, soft music playing in the background.

She knew right then that this place would be totally wasted on someone like Craig, who obsessed about profits and investments and tearing things down to build something commercial and lucrative in its place. It was too bad she couldn't afford to buy a place like this herself. She'd been raised on a farm and hated city living. She could see herself making this big, neglected farmhouse into something beautiful.

"Bobbie!" Craig called from somewhere in the back of the house. "C'mon back here. You've gotta see this view!"

Her feet suddenly unsteady, Bobbie pushed some long, raven-black hair away from her face and ambled slowly down the long, scuffed hall.

***

Ice plowed into his double cheeseburger while watching the blond babe coming out of the eatery and sashaying over to the other side of the lot, where a late-model red Jag awaited her.

She wore a pink tank top and white shorts, and her legs were long and shapely. Nice stuff, he thought. The babe looked about twenty-two, and the Jag probably went for sixty or eighty K. Blondie no doubt had a serious sugar daddy providing her with her expensive toys.

Jett pulled open the passenger door of the pickup and climbed in.

"What the hell kept ya?" Ice snatched the quart bottle of Wild Turkey double-wrapped inside two brown paper bags from the boy's grasp. "You were in that damn store so long, I thought you decided to rob the place." He broke the seal, removed the cap and dropped a healthy inch or two of the warm whiskey down his throat.

"You know the trouble they give me in those places." Jett gulped down a little booze when his huge friend handed over the bottle. "I'm twenty-two now and everybody thinks I'm sixteen."

"Well, next time we need booze, I'll get it."

Jett opened his white bag and took out a bacon cheeseburger from its foil wrappings. He began chowing down, ketchup and mustard forming reddish-yellow blots sliding down the corners of his mouth and gathering on his pointed chin.

Ice had another slug of whiskey and set the bottle carefully on the cracked vinyl console between them.

The parking lot was crowded. It was just past seven, and folks were getting hungry. Ice didn't like crowds and got as antsy as a caged Doberman when he was doing a job and heavy traffic bogged everything down.

I-70 rush-hour traffic usually thinned out by now. But since it was Friday night, the assholes out for a good time would surely gum up the works. Luckily, the kid was with him. Ice didn't want to do this one by himself. For one thing, the target might not be alone—Ice had been told a chick could be involved. The photo the Man emailed to Ice's phone the other day showed she was a real looker, with a body that wouldn't quit. Ice didn't like dusting chicks, but once in a great while it had to be done. He just didn't like it when something as hot as this number had to be taken out of the picture.

But if she was there at the wrong time, he'd have no choice…

This babe—as well as the blonde with the Jag—reminded him once again how long it had been since he'd been laid. He began thinking of that spic hooker again, the one he'd bought a little more than two months ago in Pittsburgh. The woman was as fine as silk—thick black hair down to the smooth, brown globes of her ass, huge black eyes, luscious lips…

If only the bitch had kept her damned mouth shut while she was being slammed…

13

Ice had another belt of the wild stuff and turned to Jett. "I wanna check out a new place when we're done eatin' and eyeball the hookers."

"What about the job?" Jett, dripping mustard and ketchup, looked as confused as usual.

Ice sighed. The kid was all right for a total fuckup. When you're twenty-two, you're gonna be messed up—no two ways about it. However, this kid had a shitload of other problems. Ice knew something was wrong with him when he'd picked up the boy outside that Shadyside dive in the wee hours of the morning some weeks back, the kid dirty and sweaty, babbling away like he'd just escaped a psycho ward.

Ice had felt sorry for him. The kid reminded him of his little brother Lonnie, who'd died at sixteen after running away one night when Pops had wailed the shit out of both of them during one of his drunken stupors.

Lonnie just up and ran, right out the front door in the middle of a freezing storm. He'd apparently walked and walked until he couldn't walk any more. Then, half-crazy with cold and exhaustion, he lay down in the middle of the slick, frozen highway and just went blank. He was out cold and frozen stiff when an oil tanker, driven by a dazed trucker on bennies highballing it to make a deadline, ran over him at three A.M. the next morning.

This kid Jett resembled Lonnie so much that Ice had nearly totaled the pickup that night when he'd grinded to a stop to have a closer look. For the longest time he just sat behind the wheel, gazing at the boy while remembering his brother. It wasn't

14

that Jett actually *looked* like Lonnie... It was the slender build—the way the boy tilted his head to one side when he walked. It was the way he always looked down, keeping his hands buried in his pockets.

Just like Lonnie.

Ice caught Jett having a bad dream one night when they were sacked out under the stars in the bed of the pickup. The kid was whimpering like a whipped puppy, mumbling about some guy named Reagan staying away, that he didn't want him near them anymore.

The kid would be okay with someone looking after him. Once Ice had gotten him away from his old lady, the kid began to come around. It wasn't natural, a kid Jett's age living with his old lady, a used-up hooker going to bed with the bottle because her johns started chasing younger, fresher tail.

"What about the job?" Jett had asked.

"We got all night. I heard this Wheeling place has got some dynamite hookers. Once we do the job, we'll come back here and have some fun. The man gave me five grand as a down payment. We're gettin' a hundred K for this hit, twenty-five more if the chick's with him and we do her without a hitch. That's good money, no matter how ya slice it up. Right-o?"

"Right-o, Ice." Jett grinned and belched loudly.

Ice had another belt of whiskey.

Tons of money could be made in this line of work. You could settle for just one or two hits a year and live damn good—as Ice had been doing the last five years. When this one was finished, he'd head on down to Daytona Beach, soak up some sun and do a couple of hot biker babes while it was still off-season.

"No reason why we can't have a little fun, is there?"

"No siree, Ice," Jett said, chewing the rest of his cheeseburger.

Chapter 2 - 7:15 P.M.

Craig had the refrigerator wide open when she slipped through the kitchen doorway. "Sit." He jerked his head toward the breakfast nook. "Stay a while."

Sighing tiredly, Bobbie lowered herself onto the padded cushion.

"You could've left your bag in the Porsche, you know."

"I felt like bringing it in with me."

"Whatever."

She watched him for a few moments, wondering what he was doing. Then, deciding it wasn't important, she turned toward the bay window. Twenty feet beyond it, the winding dirt drive led to the barn. An aluminum shed sat next to the barn. A stack of cordwood piled four feet high covered the side of the shed.

Craig came over to where she sat at the window. "That cordwood was left from the last winter the Gelts spent here, when the old man had his heart attack."

A homemade barbecue grill fashioned from concrete blocks and covered with a thick wrought-iron grill sat a few feet from front of the shed. About sixty feet from the rear porch, a three-car block garage sat at the end of the drive. Just beyond the barn, a fenced paddock extended into the pine trees covering the side of the hill. By the looks of it, Bobbie figured it had been built many years ago.

Half the posts were down, the slats weathered and beat-up.

The boarded-up kitchen door led to the rear porch. The door leading from the porch was closed up with crisscrossed one-by-fours as well.

"The realtor paid one of the locals to board up the back," Craig said. "Vandals seem to find their way out here in the country as well as in the city."

"It's a nice view." Bobbie liked the pastoral feel and sensed that she'd gone back in time. This place reminded her so much of the farm where she grew up. "How much property is this?"

"This place is a little more than sixty acres. I bought it and an adjoining parcel at an estate auction several months ago. When Old Man Gelt died, he left a lot of bills. His widow moved back to Shadyside. Most of her family lives in the city."

Bobbie said nothing as Craig went back to have another look in the refrigerator. She was more interested in the view out back. For a little while, at least, her discomfort had disappeared. She gazed at the tall pines near the dirt path leading to the barn. She could visualize them covered with clumps of snow and imagined one of them decorated and standing in a corner of the living room for Christmas.

Her most fondly remembered years were spent in a rented farmhouse. Her energies back then were devoted to climbing trees, fishing, skiing, and exploring the thirty acres of woodlands behind the property. She clearly remembered the times she'd been torn from her fun-filled adventures by her mother's shouting from the back porch, announcing supper was ready. "It's a shame," she said softly, almost to herself.

Craig came back over. "What's a shame?"

"A woman lost her husband and then her home in a very short time." She couldn't help feeling genuine disgust that a man as intelligent as Craig couldn't figure this out on his own.

He patted her shoulder. "Gelt was seventy-five. His widow literally hustled ass to get this deal ready for the block. She didn't want to hang on to the place. She wanted to be back with her relatives."

A few copper-brown October leaves scattered from the trees as the cool evening wind swooped down from the west. Despite her anger for letting Craig bring her here, Bobbie was starting to get a real feel for this place. The back yard certainly looked interesting. The hill beyond the paddock went on forever, turning into a tree-covered mountainside a few hundred yards in the distance.

She remembered the time when, as a little girl, she pulled her sled up the steep path to begin a full-scale assault back down the hill, to the snow-covered clearing below, where Judy and some neighborhood kids anxiously waited, teeth chattering, snowballs carefully packed and tightly clenched inside snow-encrusted mittens.

"I feel sorry for anyone who suffers a personal loss," she said softly, gazing outside.

"Don't let it worry you. The widow's perfectly happy. And that's enough talk, okay? What say you and I check the rest of the house? We can start by having a look upstairs."

19

Bobbie stiffened. "I thought you wanted me to see the property."

"I figured you'd want to see the house first."

"The property is what you bought—right?"

"Well, yes...but as I told you, I'd like to convert the house into a store, or maybe an old-style restaurant for tourists."

"So why do I need to see the upstairs?"

"I want you to see the whole thing. The big picture."

She didn't reply.

"You seem...suspicious."

"There's a good reason for that."

"Your expression tells me that we obviously need to clear the air."

"You're certainly right about that..."

He stared at her for several moments before speaking. "What exactly are you talking about?"

"It's the idea of bringing me here at this time of day to check out a piece of property. You know it's soon gonna be too dark for me to see anything, right?"

"That last board meeting went way too long. I really couldn't help that. I told you that and I already apologized."

"Then why didn't you wait until Monday to bring me out here?"

"Bobbie, I wish you'd tell me what's on your mind."

"You really want to know?"

"Yes. I really do."

She took a breath. "You brought me out here to look at the place. Once I've done what you've

20

asked, you promised to take me back to town. But now you want to take me upstairs, and you know as well as I do that there's really no reason in the world why I need to look at anything up there."

His face instantly paled, telling her he knew he'd screwed up.

"Are you gonna deny that you want to have an affair with me?"

His face remained pale. He stared at her for the longest time before turning away. Then he sighed. "No."

"Why, Craig? You're married."

He turned back in her direction, and she could see the blankness. Then he said, "Colleen and I have been growing apart for years."

"So that explains your so-called 'separation?'"

"It was a mutual thing. We'd been having problems."

"Really?"

"Of course. Don't you believe me?"

"Why should I when you've been lying to me? Is that the truth? Is Colleen really a stone bitch? The "Ice Princess," as you like calling her?"

"You don't live with the woman."

"It doesn't matter. You don't treat your wife like that."

"We haven't had sex in…in a long time."

"So that entitles you to cheat on her?" Her cheeks had suddenly become warm. She struggled to stay calm, but the man was being plain stupid. "You lied to me."

Craig didn't speak.

"What else have you lied about?"

21

"Nothing."

"You're sure?"

He nodded.

Despite her anger, she found herself feeling sorry for him. The man was a millionaire, owned a lucrative business, lived in a luxurious penthouse apartment, owned three luxury cars, a fifty-foot yacht and his own charter jet. Even so, he was a pathetic jerk.

"I guess you know now that I'm having a major problem with all this."

He stared at the table in front of him.

"I want you to drive me back."

"But you haven't seen—"

"You've brought me out here on the pretext of looking at your real estate property, but as soon as we get in the door, you're touching me and rubbing against me, and now you want me to go upstairs with you... "

He went over and yanked open the fridge door so roughly, it banged against the chipped wooden cabinet next to it. He pulled out a bottle of Chardonnay, opened it, got two glasses from the cabinet, and poured. He left one glass on the counter and went back to the nook.

Bobbie stared at him, the wine, and the glasses. He'd obviously come out here earlier—which told her that this 'spur-of-the-moment' trip had been well-planned. "I see you've got the fridge well-stocked."

Craig took a healthy swig, lowered the glass and looked her right in the eye. "I knew I was coming here. I've got to check things out, don't I?"

"*That's* why there's wine in the fridge?"

"Why else would there be?"

"You really don't want me to answer that, do you?"

He looked hurt. "Don't tell me you think I—"

"You must think I'm an idiot."

"On the contrary. I know how smart you are. Why else do you think I hired you?"

"You honestly don't want me to answer *that*, either…"

He studied his wine glass. "I really think a lot of you."

"I'll just bet you do."

"Listen…we need to talk about this."

She turned away. The man had already dug his hole. Now he was making it bigger so he could pull her in it with him.

"C'mon. Let's go upstairs. I promise we'll just check out the rooms, then we can—"

"You haven't been listening to a word I've said, and I'm sick and tired of it." She got up and squeezed past him.

"*Dammit*…" He groped clumsily for her hand.

She pulled away.

He tried again, succeeding this time.

Frightened and angry, Bobbie felt the panic closing in on her. Without thinking, she hauled off and slapped the man sharply across the face.

***

Fancy Dan's was hopping by seven-thirty that evening.

Located in the heart of downtown Wheeling, the well-known bar was the prime hangout for the

23

best-looking hookers in the area. The clientele ranged from blue-collar locals to white-collar tourists. Fancy Dan's wasn't known for its elegance or high-class appearance. However, its heavy nightly traffic didn't go there to enjoy its furnishings or atmosphere.

As Ice puffed on his Marlboro and watched the nervous activity at the bar's front entrance, he thought about the old days, when he'd busted his hump ten hours a day, bent over an engine or squeezed beneath a chassis, fucking up his back, neck, and knuckles for fifteen lousy bucks an hour. Meanwhile, his wife Gina had her hair and nails done and watched soaps when she wasn't out spending the rest of his hard-earned money at the local lingerie shops, or at the liquor store for her fancy high-priced wines.

This went on for four years before the uppity bitch got bored with home life and started opening her thighs—first, for the cable hookup man, then the well-dressed computer analyst from Youngstown who'd seen her sunning in the front yard in one of her scanty Italian-made two-pieces and stopped to ask for directions.

Now, as he sat in the pickup outside Fancy Dan's, sizing up the whores, he thought about Gina and how little she'd actually mattered in the great scheme of things.

"How much do these ladies cost, Ice?" Jett asked.

"Kid, once we get paid for this gig, we'll be able to buy every damn hooker that just walked into that place."

24

"The redhead, too?"

Ice had seen Jett eyeballing the redhead earlier. And she wasn't bad—not even to Ice, who'd seen better whores at the Greyhound Bus Terminal. She had long legs, and her thick rusty locks covered her shoulders and back. And the valley between those big jugs was deep enough to bury your head inside.

"Kid, you slip that redhead a C-note or two, she's gonna be all over you."

Jett laughed nervously.

"Ready to go inside?"

Jett suddenly seemed serious. "Ice, tell me about this job again. I wanna make sure I got everything figured out right."

Ice tossed his spent cigarette out the window. "You don't need to know. I'm handlin' things."

"I just don't wanna mess anything up."

"All you need to know is that we're gettin' a hundred K to go to this dude's country place and put out his lights. If he's got a babe with him, there's a bonus of another twenty-five K if we do her, too."

"Sounds pretty easy."

"Normally, it would be."

"What makes this different?"

"There can't be any trace of foul play."

"Really?"

"It has to look like an accident."

Chapter 3 - 7:45 P.M.

Cursing herself for she'd just done, Bobbie waited nervously outside the kitchen bathroom.

She was more worried that she'd hurt him rather than she was about losing her job. After all, she'd put most of her strength into that swat. She just hoped she hadn't broken the skin of his cheek with one of her nails.

Most of all, she was angry with herself for hitting him. She *never* physically assaulted people; it went against her nature. Even when she found out that Taylor was cheating just weeks after their wedding, she tried working out their problems as civilly as she could. And when she finally discovered that no amount of talking in the world would fix Taylor's uncontrollable fascination with every attractive female he ever ran across, she merely filed for divorce and went her own way.

But even though Taylor deserved a wakeup call more than anyone else she'd ever met, she'd *never* physically assaulted the man.

After ten minutes, she decided to check on how he was doing. "Craig? You okay?"

A muffled, incomprehensible grumble resonated softly from the other side of the door.

"*What* was that?"

"I said, *I'm okay*, dammit."

"Is there any…blood? I mean, did my nails—"

"*No*."

26

The door opened. He slipped past her and headed straight for the kitchen counter. His face was flushed with anger and embarrassment, but she couldn't see any marks or welts where she'd slugged him.

"I'm really sorry, Craig. I didn't mean to—"

"Stop it." He filled his glass and chugged down half. "I'll live."

"I really didn't mean to...that is, I don't usually do things like that."

He had more wine but didn't reply.

"I didn't want to...*hurt* you..."

He blinked. "Really?"

"Of course not. I...it was just a reflex..."

"A *reflex*?"

She nodded.

"Let me let you in on a bit of useful information you'll obviously need in the near future. You haul off and slap a guy square in the face, don't tell him it was just a reflex and expect him to jump up and do the happy dance."

Her anger had softened somewhat, but she was still determined to hold her ground. The man had lied about his wife and had been hitting on her the last six months. "You...kind of...asked for it."

"What?"

"You were *grabbing* me..." She wanted to justify her actions but knew it would sound lame, no matter what she said. "You just wouldn't listen."

"So that gives you the right to *slap* me?"

"I didn't know what else to do."

"You couldn't have just told me to back off?"

"Are you saying that would have actually *worked*?"

"You might have at least *tried* it, rather than resorting to physical violence…"

She stared at the floor and wondered how she could get him to see the truth the way she saw it.

He drained his drink and poured more.

Bobbie continued staring at the floor, hating him, hating herself, hating this house. She wanted to be at home in her apartment, relaxing on the couch while sipping a good, stiff drink. She didn't want to be here in this house with this man, who'd practically stolen the place from a heartbroken old woman who'd just lost her husband.

She couldn't help it that the wrong men were attracted to her. She'd been on this same road before, and it always led to the same end. Her failed marriage and countless wrecked relationships were living proof that she'd let herself be chosen rather than waited for the right time to choose the right guy.

It didn't seem right that someone like her, who'd started life with good parents, great genes, and high intelligence, should end up in a strange farmhouse at night, watching a rich married man drain a bottle of wine.

"What's this sudden aversion you have for me?" He lowered himself onto the padded window seat and stared at the glass he'd placed on the table in front of him.

"It's not so sudden." There was no sense lying at this stage of the game. "A lot of things have been bothering me."

28

"What the hell's the problem? If it's Colleen, I'm sorry. I didn't think, dammit. I'm like that, sometimes. All men are." He ran a hand through his thinning chestnut hair. "Put yourself in my shoes. You're head of a software company, and you've been living with a woman who turned cold months earlier. One day, this gorgeous young woman walks into your place for a job, and suddenly nothing else in the world matters. You feel more alive and more vigorous than you've felt in a long, long time." He shook his head. "But you know nothing will happen because you're married. This young lady has got principles. She knows you're married and won't go near you. It's not that she's *said* anything about it, but you can sense it. This girl is much too classy for that. And you've seen your best friend, Jerry, the world's biggest player, land flat on his face every time he even attempts to deliver a line to this lady."

Bobbie wanted to tell him she thought Jerry Van Dusen was revolting and obnoxious but didn't think that would matter.

"So you make up stories and hope this lady believes you and feels sorry for you. It helps that you've been having marital problems, so you work it from that angle and hope it eventually comes together. And if it doesn't, you create opportunities to get this lady alone with you. Hell, you own the damned company—how difficult would it be to get her to go with you to the airport? Or to a business luncheon? Or to a place in the country, where you just bought several parcels of prime farmland for a real estate investment?" He went silent and gazed out the back window.

29

Bobbie thought about what the man had just said. He sounded sincere—which made it worse. It only made him more of an arrogant, selfish jerk who wanted to cheat on his wife. "That doesn't make this right."

"Maybe not, but it's the truth."

"I can't forgive you for it."

"I understand."

"Do you?"

"I don't like it. But yes, I understand."

"If only you could see it the way I do."

He sighed. "I'm a man. I gave you the story from my perspective so you could see it the way I do. But you can't because you're a woman." He shrugged. "And that's the problem, isn't it?"

"That's not it at all."

"What *is* it, then?"

She stared at the window behind him. When she saw the blackness of the night approaching, she sensed a looming terror she hadn't expected. Would she have to venture out into that cold, unfamiliar blackness all alone? Or would he put his anger and humiliation behind him and do the gentlemanly thing? Craig Sheffield was an extremely successful, sophisticated man. However, she'd been in the work force for nearly five years and already knew quite a bit about the rich. They knew all about the best foods, the best wines, the best caviar, the best cars, the best places for a vacation and the best and most efficient ways to invest huge amounts of money... But when they were insulted, wronged or embarrassed, they reacted like anyone else. And the richer they were, the nastier they reacted.

She'd just slapped a rich man in the face and told him she didn't want him. Expecting him to tell her to walk back to Wheeling, at this point, would not be much of a stretch.

But she couldn't let that intimidate or influence her in any way. Her pride and self-respect were what mattered. All things considered, it really wasn't that crucial how she got home. If worse came to worse, she could use her cell and get a cab out here. It would be pricey, but if she had no other choice, she'd just have to bite the bullet...

"Well?" He was waiting for an explanation. "What is it?"

"The problem is me. I have to be more in control of my life."

He picked up his glass and took a healthy slug. He was quiet for a few moments. Then he sent over a cold look that made her skin flush. "What's all this nonsense I've been hearing about Jerry? If he's treated you badly in any way—"

"It's not the way he treats me. It's the way he looks at me."

"I know he's tried hitting on you. I saw him do it a couple of times."

Her pulse raced when she recalled the insinuations Van Dusen had made at company luncheons, his hurtful remarks when he'd caught her alone in the elevator. She took a breath. "It was more than a couple of times."

He scowled. "When was the last time he did it?"

"It's been a while."

"And just how does he look at you?"

31

She shrugged. "It's hard to explain—"

"Try."

She could tell by his fierce expression that he wasn't going to let her off the hook. "A girl notices certain things. It's like…like he wants to—"

"He wants to get in your pants. It's that simple."

"I don't think it's that at all."

"I'd really appreciate it if you told me what the hell's going on…"

"I know the difference between a guy who wants me and a guy who hates me because his partner also wants me."

"So, you think this is jealousy? A simple rivalry thing?"

"It could be…"

"You're way off-base with that one. You just don't know Jerry. He's been in heat since he was eight years old. With women, he forgets about everything—including partners. And when a hot, beautiful babe like you enters the picture, he simply loses all perspective."

Bobbie sighed. Could she ever convince him she was right about this? She knew how guys were when a woman came into the picture. It changed everything. They began dressing differently, acting differently, speaking differently. They did silly things and reverted back to their adolescence, when the homecoming queen passed in the hall and turned in their direction.

But would Craig even understand this? Even if he did, he wouldn't admit it. Not to her, anyway…

"Women…know stuff like that," she said finally.

"Let's forget about Jerry. He's my friend and my partner, but like I just said, he's constantly in heat, and anyway, I didn't come here to talk about him."

"No. You came here to cheat on your wife."

"Dammit…" He reached for his wine glass.

"Put yourself in Colleen's shoes. She has feelings. We all do."

"So do men."

"It's different with men."

"How?"

She wondered if he was serious. It bothered her that he hadn't learned much about women even though he was approaching forty and had obviously been involved with women for more than half his life. But since he'd asked, she was going to tell him and wasn't going to pull any punches. "Men don't feel emotions as deeply as women. They don't hurt as badly. Women feel hurt down to their soul. And when something comes between them and the man they love, they can feel it. They sense when something's missing…when something's changed. With a woman, love is a tangible entity. When it changes in any way, it affects them very deeply. For a woman, losing love is just as horrible as losing a loved one."

"What if there was nothing there to begin with?"

She gazed at him, looking for some sign of humanity…of decency. "There must've been something…once."

He finished the wine and thumped the glass down. He seemed more agitated than just moments before. "Women know this, they know that. They know when their husbands are messing around, when their lover's partner knows who's banging who. When a guy wants in their pants—"

"Stop it." She could tell the wine was making him even more obnoxious.

"If I don't, are you gonna slap me again?"

She turned away and saw more darkness peering at her from the back window.

He got up and lumbered unsteadily to the doorway. "I'm going out for a walk. I need some fresh air."

Robbie stiffened. This situation was getting worse by the moment. "When are we going back to Wheeling?"

"In a bit. I can't drive after I've done all this drinking."

"*I* can drive—"

He forced out a laugh. "You actually think I'm going to let you or anyone else drive that Porsche?"

"Craig, I need to get back home…"

Without another word, he turned and staggered out of the room. His footsteps were heavy and uneven on the floorboards in the hall.

The screen door banged shut.

***

Jett couldn't stop staring at the redhead sitting in the corner, smoking a cigarette, and drinking out of a frosted glass with a funny green umbrella sticking out of it. She sat with her right leg crossed over the left, her foot keeping up with the beat thumping from the jukebox.

34

She sure looked good—real classy. She had nice legs and really big tits. Her flaming red hair came down in a full sweep to her low-cut top, where the swell of her tits formed a valley a foot deep.

Jett felt a warm rush. It was like somebody had just dumped a glass of hot water in his lap. His momma used to wear similar outfits when she was working in those places Jett wasn't allowed inside. Momma had a special way of moving when she was working. She shifted her hips a certain way, arching her back and tilting her head to make her hair slide down her shoulder. Her clothes were just as fancy as the duds these ladies were wearing. No one looked better than Momma when she was all dolled up—jewelry dangling from her wrists and neck and ears, her wig brushed and sprayed, her sweet-smelling perfume dabbed on her neck and between her breasts.

Ice came back from the room marked *Dudes* and sat down.

"I want her," Jett said, his full attention on her.

Ice frowned. "Not now, kid." He sucked down a slug of beer. "We'll head on out there and do the job. *Then* we can come back for Red."

"She's doin' a number on me, Ice." Jett squirmed in his chair.

"I seen better, kid."

Ice just didn't understand.

"I *want* her, Ice…"

Ice's cold blue eyes instantly turned mean.

Jett sat back awkwardly in his chair and hoped the big man didn't throw a fit. He'd seen Ice angry just a few days ago. When that Indian cashier guy at the 7-Eleven shortchanged them after they'd just bought gas and a twelve-pack, Ice grabbed the dark, lanky man by the white shirt collar, lifting him up and over the counter, as though the Indian didn't weigh much more than the twelve-pack they'd just taken out of the refrigerator.

It had taken Jett a while to get Ice to chill out. Ice eventually calmed down, but Jett would never forget how quickly the big man had moved, twisting and jerking his two hundred and fifty-odd pounds like a bolt of lightning.

"You can have her later, goddammit."

Jett made one last plea. He knew he was pushing things, but this was urgent. He'd never actually been properly laid before. "What if she's busy...when we get back?"

Ice stood up quickly, his left boot forcing his chair back and slamming it against the table behind them. Three large blue-collar workers sat at the table, getting plastered on boilermakers. They'd straightened when Ice's jerking had nearly spilled their pitcher. All three began to stand but took one long look at Ice's broad back and huge tattooed arms and decided to ignore the minor disturbance.

Ice marched right over to the redhead's table. His back was to Jett, but the boy could see Ice reaching into the back pocket of his denims, taking out some bills and dropping them on her table.

The redhead smiled briefly and stuffed the bills down her cleavage.

Ice came back, sat down, and picked up his beer.

"Wh-What'd ya do?" Jett asked.

36

"Gave her some cash." Ice finished his beer. "Trust me. She'll be here when we get back."

Jett couldn't remember Momma doing business this way. It didn't seem likely that it would work. "Ya *really* think she'll be here when we get back?"

Ice sucked down some cigarette smoke. "Better be. I forked over four hundred. Two C-notes for her and two for her friend—the blonde standin' over there by the juke. Told Red we'd be here tomorrow night, same time. They can do what they want till then, but when we come back, they better be available. Told 'em there's a grand in it for each."

Jett grinned.

"I also told her we better not have to come lookin' for 'em."

"What'd she say?"

"Just gave me one of those looks broads give when they're about to piss themselves."

Jett knew what the big man meant.

A taut look took over Ice's broad face when he chugged the rest of his beer, put down the empty bottle and got up from the table. "Let's go earn some big money, kid."

Chapter 4 - 8:15 P.M.

Bobbie sat at the breakfast nook, feeling despondent and alone.

The weekend was shot, no matter how she looked at it. Craig would eventually come back angry from the argument and the humiliation from her slapping him...and probably still just as drunk from the wine.

She hoped he wouldn't want to try anything again. Even though he was slightly drunk, he knew better. The man couldn't possibly be so desperate that he'd lost all his self-respect.

Anyway, he had more important issues to contend with. She refused to believe he had no conscience. He had to know that he couldn't possibly justify what he'd done, how he'd made her feel. He'd lied to her and tricked her for a night of sex.

But right now, he had to know that she didn't want any part of it. Even an idiot could tell that all she wanted was to get out of here. Craig was no idiot; he knew that the only thing in her mind was to drive back to her place, where her private world of peace and quiet awaited her. She wanted all this—and, of course, to try and forget what had happened. And also decide how she could leave the company without hurting her chances for a future in software.

Yes, it had finally come to that. She couldn't see herself working for a man she could not possibly respect or trust.

She pulled her cell out of her bag and tried turning it on. The cursed words—*LOW BATTERY*—sent chills up her spine. *Damn you, Bobbie Marsh…you've done it again!* She cursed herself for forgetting to charge it properly.

How many times had she done that same stupid thing? Ten? Twenty? It didn't matter, did it? The damage was done.

Normally, she charged it the moment she came home. She couldn't remember why she hadn't done it yesterday evening. She might have had other things on her mind. But it didn't matter, because right this moment she really needed it to work, and because it didn't, this situation could turn horribly bad. Craig might simply get in his Porsche and drive back to Wheeling. She'd be stranded in the middle of nowhere, miles from the closest road and at the mercy of any killer or predatory animal that happened her way.

With a deep sigh, she rubbed her temples and tried thinking of some way to soften things—and getting back in his good graces—at least for the time being.

***

Slouched behind the wheel of the pickup, Ice watched the tall, slender figure moving around in front of the big farmhouse.

Ice had parked in the middle of a cluster of high bushes about twenty feet off the dirt road where the path split, the right fork turning into a wooded ledge about two hundred feet down from the front porch.

Ice had spent the day before last driving around out here, checking out the terrain and the surrounding areas for key checkpoints and landmarks. He'd learned years ago, when he'd first started dusting people for cash, that getting to know the terrain was of paramount importance. This way, you always had the edge because you knew where your quarry might hide or what path he'd use to attempt an escape.

"That him, Ice?" Jett whispered.

Despite the dim haze from the floodlights highlighting the front porch of the farmhouse, Ice recognized the neat hairdo, the high forehead and the slim build.

"Quiet," he whispered back. "Want the bastard to hear you? The air's moving directly toward the house."

Jett went silent.

The night had become thick and dark, mostly because of the tall pines surrounding the property. The floods bolted to the underside of the porch roof splashed the front steps with a bright shade of yellow gauze that reached the glittering paint job of the silver Porsche parked out front.

Head lowered, hands in pockets, Mr. Big Shot stood in front of the house at least a full minute before turning around and disappearing around the corner.

"Sit tight and keep quiet." Ice wanted to observe some more and see if he could get a glimpse of a chick.

Jett made no comment.

Mr. Big Shot was out of sight for about ten minutes. When he appeared again, he was moving sluggishly. He looked like he'd just had a few. He stopped at the corner of the house, bent his head back and gazed up at the dark sky. After about a minute, he lowered his head. Then he turned back to the house and went up the front steps, using the rickety wooden rail to keep himself from falling.

Yep, Mr. Big Shot had definitely had a few.

Ice grinned. This was gonna be a piece of cake…

41

Chapter 5 - 8:30 P.M.

Bobbie got up from the kitchen nook and went over to the doorway.

Craig had been gone more than half an hour, and she was getting nervous. She wanted to get away from this place, and if he was too drunk to drive, she'd have to take the keys from him. This was insane. She didn't even want to be here, and she certainly wasn't going to stay here for the night just because Craig was too drunk to drive and too stubborn to give her his keys.

Just then, he opened the screen door.

She watched him, noting how tired and drawn his face looked in the hall lighting. But that didn't really matter. What mattered was that she had to take control and get him to start thinking rationally. "We really need to get back to town. It's late and I have to get home, and if you're too drunk, you're going to let me drive, and I don't care how you feel about it, or—"

"I'm all right, I guess."

"You're sure?"

"I'm sure, dammit."

"You're able to drive?"

"Of course I'm able to drive."

She could tell he was much more upset than drunk—which told her he had no business getting behind the wheel of a car. But in his present state, he wouldn't surrender his keys to anyone— especially a woman who'd just slapped him in the face and told him she didn't want to have anything to do with him.

"I don't think you are…"

"I really don't *care* what you think."

She told herself that above everything else, she shouldn't lose her reserve. She couldn't let him win this round. She wanted her life back, and if she had to physically get his keys away from him, she was going to do it. "Your opinion of me doesn't matter anymore. All I care about is getting back to town. I don't want to be out here with you any longer."

His head dropped, like a stage curtain at the end of a play. He began looking at his feet.

Bobbie felt a wave of disgust. There was something pathetic about a grown man standing like that. He looked like a small boy left alone in a crowded store, parents nowhere in sight.

Even so, she knew this wasn't her fault. The man had put her in a position she didn't want to be in. It didn't matter that he was married, or that he and his wife were having problems. He had no business bringing her here under false pretenses.

"So that's it, then?" He was staring at her again. The pathetic quality had gone. It sounded like he'd processed his anger and started thinking logically.

"I really would like it if we left right now. Would you mind?"

"Of course not."

"You're sure?"

"I'm sure."

"I'd appreciate it."

"At least you got to see the house."

"It's a very nice place. You should be able to do a lot of great things with it, as well as with the property."

"Right now, I think I'll just sit on it and sell it when the prices go back up in the spring."

"Whatever you want to do." She wanted to check the time again. She knew it must be getting close to nine by now.

"Or I could stick with the golf course idea..."

She forced a smile. She didn't want him to see the impatience on her face. It would probably set him off again. "As I just said, it's a very nice place and has a slew of possibilities. Thanks for showing it to me."

He stared at her for nearly a minute before speaking. "What about your future at Sheffwares? You don't intend to quit just because—"

"We'll talk about that later, okay?" She didn't want to upset him further by telling him her Sheffwares days were over. Her longing to get out of here and drive back home had become overwhelming. She couldn't think of anything else.

He fidgeted a little, shifting his weight. He said something about turning off all the lights and locking up.

"I need to use the bathroom first."

He nodded tiredly. "I'll give you a few minutes."

"Thank you."

He turned and went back outside.

***

44

Squinting behind a pair of expensive binoculars, Ice watched Mr. Big Shot pacing the front porch as if something was bothering him.

Then he stopped and turned toward the front door—as if he was waiting for something. Or someone. About two minutes later, he plodded down the porch steps and went over to the Porsche.

"Gun's under the seat, with the tape," he whispered, risking a quick glance at Jett. "Looks like it's time to rock 'n roll."

"What about the lady?"

"I haven't even seen her yet."

"But if she's inside—"

"Just get the gun and the tape, dammit."

The boy felt around beneath the seat and found the revolver—a Taurus .38 Police Special Ice had bought the week before at a Pittsburgh hock shop. The gun was old but worked and would do just fine. Ice had taken it out to an open field a couple of days ago to try it out. It did what it was supposed to and didn't even have much of a kick. Ice had spent that same night cleaning and oiling the gun, as well as filing off the serial number. He'd decided not to wrap the trigger, guard, and grip with masking tape, as he customarily did.

This one had to be done strictly as ordered. Since he was told not to use the gun in the first place, there was no need to take such precautions. The gun would be used to hold on Mr. Big Shot while Jett taped him up. Then Ice and Jett would haul him back to the house, place him on the living room couch and smother him. They'd remove the tape and build a roaring fire in the fireplace with the flue closed tight.

Jett handed over the gun.

Ice stuck it under his wide leather belt. "Open your door real careful and leave it open. No noise, right?"

"Right, Ice."

They disappeared silently in the darkness of the night.

46

Chapter 6 - 8:45 P.M.

Rustling in the bushes just twenty feet away made Craig stop cold. His pulse racing, he jerked his head toward the sound.

The overgrown bushes lining the far side of the dirt drive told him nothing. The porch lights shed a film of hazy light over the car and about ten feet beyond, forming vague gold bands resting on the roof of the car and splashing the tops of the bushes at the crest of the hill descending sharply to the road nearly a hundred yards below.

As his vision acclimated itself to the dark, he was aware of a shiny horizontal outline down the path behind the trees. A slender Frisbee-shaped object hovered there, its yellowy crescent shape just above the bushes. His imagination instantly grasped the most far-fetched possibilities.

A flying saucer?

Bobbie has got me so messed up, I don't even know my own name. Now I'm imagining all sorts of crazy things...

The eeriness of the night poked at him, and he remembered Bobbie's comment about the place looking haunted.

What if that really is *a flying saucer? What if—*

Reality nudged him, forcing him to think more clearly.

If it isn't a saucer, what the hell is it? The roof of a vehicle?

A truck, maybe?

But what would a truck be doing out here?

He heard something else, this time in the opposite direction. Once again his mind, jumpy and frightened, thought of the fantastic.

Little green men?

Damn you, Bobbie. You might have slapped me pretty damned hard, but it sure as hell wasn't hard enough to scramble my brains!

He shook himself. The damned Chardonnay…it wasn't helping matters…

More rustling. He jerked toward the sound just in time to catch movement near the corner of the house, just out of range of the floods.

"S-Someone…out here?" His voice was shaky—which was no wonder. The fear had sent a cold chill racing up his back. His jittery hand had slipped from the door handle of the Porsche and went for his jacket pocket, where he kept his cell phone.

His mind once again blurred with crazy images. He recalled someone at the auction mentioning that the sheer isolation of the Gelt house made it susceptible to horror stories. And the dark night sure didn't help matters. The cool wind whispering through the trees sent shivers up his spine.

If only I hadn't sucked down so much damned wine...

It was at that instant that his fear told him to get back in the house. *Now*.

He spun around sharply, on feet that had suddenly turned into blocks of ice. But thanks to Bally and the early morning jogging, his legs didn't fail him. In the next instant, he leaped for the porch

48

steps. He watched his hand reaching out for the screen door, which suddenly seemed a hundred miles away.

Something big, hot, and terribly strong grabbed him by the shirt collar. A heady stench of meat, beer and very rank sweat assaulted his nostrils the same moment he was picked up from the ground and jerked backwards.

He made a feeble attempt to pull away, but the grip on him was unyielding. Everything went hazy and seemed far away, as though he was looking through the wrong end of a pair of binoculars. Then something huge and solid wrapped itself around his neck, and his air was choked off. He hadn't even had time to force out a decent gasp.

He had one last thought of Bobbie in her tight jeans and pullover sweater…

Blackness swallowed him up.

***

Bobbie came out of the bathroom, glanced at the screen door, and froze.

Shadows were moving around out front.

Gripping her handbag, she crept cautiously down the hall and, standing to the side of the screen door, peered out.

Shadows were moving in front of Craig's Porsche.

The back of her head grew cold and tingly. It felt like drops of ice water trickling down her neck.

Several things registered at once. She wondered, at first, if the shadow was Craig…why he was running outside in the dark. Then she considered the possibility that he could be chasing someone—or some*thing*—that had turned up in the front yard.

A stray dog? Perhaps a raccoon, or possum, had come out of the bushes. The animal could have frightened him. And Craig, not exactly thinking clearly, had taken off after it.

Or maybe it was something else…

Her mind didn't want to think of this, but somehow, she just couldn't force it out of her head.

Maybe someone—or some*thing*—was chasing *him*.

This made no sense. They were out in the middle of nowhere, for one thing. No one knew they were here. Perhaps she was more upset than she realized. Or maybe it was that Norman Bates thing that had been hiding in the darkest recesses of her head ever since they pulled up in front of the house. If the shadow was Craig, he'd soon be coming back inside. He'd have to come back. Once she was ready to go back, he had to turn off all the lights and lock up.

The other thought slammed through her, this time even more brutally.

What if that *wasn't* Craig out there?

The cold tingling returned, and she spun around so quickly, she nearly tripped. She dropped her handbag and jacket on the floor and tiptoed over to the tattered living room drapes, keeping to the side so she couldn't be seen.

The only lights shining were the tiny 25-watt bulb on the kitchen wall and the hall light, which lit the front entrance of the house and the first ten feet or so of the hall. She knew she should have turned off the kitchen wall light when Craig had gone outside, but she'd been upset, and had gone to the bathroom instead to wash the mascara from her streaked eyes.

Shaking a little, she pushed aside the drapes ever so slightly and peered outside.

Two figures were standing no more than ten feet from the front porch. One of the men was huge, with a shaved head and rippling muscles. The other was nearly a head shorter, and skinny. The skinny one was standing near Craig, who lay on his back on the ground.

The huge, scary one was holding a gun. It was aimed at Craig's face.

Chapter 7 - 9:00 P.M.

As Ice aimed the .38 at the man's face, he eyed the front hall at the same time.

There didn't seem to be any movement inside. Other than some light coming from another room, the hall looked empty. If someone else was inside, they were probably in a different room.

In any event, there was plenty of time to check the house.

Jett taped the man's wrists together behind his back. He then peeled off a strip about four feet long and wrapped it tightly around the man's ankles. When he'd finished, he turned to Ice. "What now, Ice?"

"We'll leave him here." Ice turned back to the well-lit hall. "We need to go inside and see if anyone else came with him. If a babe's in the house, we'll give her the same treatment. Then we'll lug this dude inside and finish up." Ice regarded Jett's work. "Don't forget the kisser."

Jett peeled off one last strip of tape and slapped it over Mr. Big Shot's mouth. Jett stood up; a serious expression had taken over his lean features. "I'm wonderin' about the fire, Ice. Won't the neighbors—"

"This is the damn country, kid. Everybody does whatever the hell they please. Nobody gives two shits about nothin'. You can probably find all sorts of nasty shit out here—dog-fightin' on Saturday nights, bodies buried all over the countryside…" He chuckled. "More perverts and psychos out here than in the city of Pittsburgh."

Jett laughed nervously.

"Anyway, by the time somebody sees the flames, we'll be long gone. This'll give the fire-boys somethin' to do, for a change."

Jett looked worried. "Won't this cause a forest fire?"

He shrugged. "St. Clairsville Fire Department's less than ten minutes from here. They handle the Belmont County area. Feel better?"

Jett nodded.

Ice bent and checked Jett's work. "That oughta hold him. Now let's go inside and check out the place."

***

As the skinny one bound Craig's wrists and ankles with tape, Bobbie told herself she was just imagining all this.

This couldn't possibly be happening.

But she knew her eyes couldn't be lying to her. This really *was* happening, and it was happening less than thirty feet away.

My God... Why are they doing this?

She couldn't just stand here, shaking like a hysterical idiot. Craig needed help. There were two of them, and one of them looked strong enough to pick up Craig's Porsche and walk away with it. But that didn't matter. She had to *do* something.

While they were both preoccupied with Craig, she snuck out into the hall and slipped through the kitchen archway. If she could somehow sneak out through the back, she might be able to find something—a block of wood, a stone—anything she could use as a weapon. Maybe she could somehow lure them away from the house and give Craig time to come to and try and free himself.

She suddenly remembered the boarded-up back door.

There was no way out but through the front.

Think, Bobbie, think!

She needed a weapon. Other than the penknife she carried in her handbag, what else did she have? But even if she could find something else, would she be able to rush out through the front and face them both?

Then she remembered the gun. She couldn't possibly go up against two men with a stupid *penknife...*

But she had to help Craig...somehow...

All thoughts were quickly dispersed when she crossed the kitchen to have another look down the hall.

Someone was on the front porch.

***

Ice stood close to the screen door, staring down the hall.

Not many lights were on. The entrance light splashed the hall, the staircase, and a portion of the rooms to the left and to the right. The room to the left was probably the living room. Another dark room sat directly across the hall, on the right.

Jett crept up to him and stood behind him, the roll of tape in his shaking hands.

Ice pressed his index finger to his lips. "If a babe's inside and she hears us, our plan's fucked.

54

All she's gotta do is get the cops on her cell and dial nine-one-one…or maybe Mr. Big Shot's got a gun somewhere in the house. We don't know what we're dealin' with yet. Follow me?"

Jett nodded.

Ice lowered his big hand and tapped Jett gently on the head. "You go on in and head down that hall. I'll stay here, near the front door, so no one slips out. The Man told me the back door's boarded up. Front's the only way out. Get the pic?"

"I think so, but—"

"But what?"

"What'll I do when—if—I find her?"

"Give a yell. Once we've got her, we don't have to be quiet anymore, right?"

Jett smiled. "Yeah."

Ice tapped him on the shoulder. "Gotta do things right, little buddy." He reached out for the rusty handle of the screen door and inched it open. "Go on in. Let's find her and wrap this up."

Jett slipped through the slim opening and moved silently down the hall.

***

Standing near the kitchen doorway, Bobbie could hear the two whispering at the screen door.

Her heart thumping madly, she snuck back into the kitchen, mashing herself flat against the plaster wall.

She was trapped, and the only way outside was through the front door, where they were standing.

The kitchen archway led into a small room.

Library? Den?

55

She hadn't noticed it until now because she hadn't paid much attention since she and Craig had come inside.

Jaw clenched, she turned awkwardly to her right.

This room was directly across the hall from the living room. If she could hide there, she might be able to circle around them when they came in. Then, with any luck, she could sneak outside, free Craig, and the two of them could try their best to get away. Hopefully, they hadn't taken Craig's cell phone. If she knew Craig, the cell would be working perfectly.

Clutching her bag and denim jacket tightly against her, Bobbie slipped through the archway and into the dark room.

A moment later, the rusty creaking of old springs emanated down the hall as the screen door opened.

***

Jett moved on tiptoe down the hall.

He stopped for a moment and turned around. Ice was outside, on the front porch. The big man urged him on, waving a huge, tattooed arm.

This was kind of scary. There could be a chick somewhere in this house and she could have a knife, or even a gun.

Best be as quiet as he could.

He stopped at the doorway in the hall and gazed into the living room. The room was dark. The hall lighting barely illuminated the front half of the room. To his right was another room, which looked smaller and even darker than the living room. There wasn't much furniture—just a table against the far wall, beneath the window.

The light coming from the kitchen made him wonder if he should check it first. It was the only lighted room on the floor. The chick could be in there, fixing something to eat. He didn't smell food but knew that didn't mean anything. She might be fixing a sandwich. Sandwiches didn't smell that strong unless you were using braunschweiger, or those smelly cheeses. If she was fixing a sandwich, he could sneak up on her when she was at the counter. Since she'd be preoccupied, he could force her to the floor and get her hands taped behind her before she knew what was happening.

Ice would be so pleased.

The tape gripped tightly in his fist, Jett continued silently down the hall.

***

Barely breathing, Bobbie kept her body mashed against the wall as one of them moved quietly down the hall.

She used all her strength and willpower to choke down the scream fighting its way out of her throat. It was tough, but she forced it right down.

She wanted to peer around the corner but knew the big one with the tattoos and the gun was still out on the porch. She figured he was standing there to make sure no one escaped.

Then she wondered if they even knew about her in the first place.

First, get away. Then you'll have all the time in the world to think things out...

57

The skinny one would probably check the kitchen first. She didn't think it would be long—ten seconds, if she was lucky—before he realized no one was in there. Then he'd stick his head in here.

Her options were severely limited. She was going to have to make a major decision very shortly.

***

Ice continued watching as the boy moved carefully down the hall, his head tilted as he took short, silent steps.

The kid was listening. Good deal.

Ice was damn proud. If this job went without a hitch, there would be another right off. The Man had mentioned something about using him again.

No harm in making more jack before he and Jett split the County, was there?

Jett disappeared in the kitchen.

Ice suddenly heard something that sounded like it had come from somewhere near the front of the house, where they'd left Mr. Big Shot.

The hairs on the back of his bull neck bristling, Ice backed away from the screen door and turned around.

Mr. Big Shot had rolled away from the Porsche and toward the front of the house, at the corner. He lay on his side, working his taped wrists against the edge of the bricks lining the flower bed.

Dammit, I should've used more muscle putting the fucker to sleep...

His huge hands curling into claws, Ice hopped off the porch.

***

Bobbie peered cautiously at the doorway.

The big shadow had moved away from the screen door.

It made her heart leap.

In that next instant, she saw something out of the corner of her eye. A shadow outside was moving past the front porch, where Craig lay helpless on the ground.

Oh my God...

Bobbie found herself facing a desperate dilemma. Should she rush outside and try and rescue Craig? Or save herself by getting away?

Could she get away?

The Porsche was parked directly out front—could she get to it?

No. She realized at once how fruitless that thought was. Craig had the keys. He always had the keys. The Porsche was his pride and joy—his "two-hundred-thousand-dollar present to myself," as he so fondly called it. Everyone who knew Craig realized how cautious and possessive he was with his toys. He'd never leave his keys in the ignition—especially out in the middle of nowhere.

But was she so certain he'd pocketed them? Yes. Of course he had. And if so, the two who'd attacked him now had them in their possession. If they didn't, they sure were stupid.

But even if Craig *had* left the keys in the ignition, she knew she couldn't possibly run outside, leap down the steps, yank open the car door, jump inside, start it up, slam it in reverse and tear down the dirt drive before that big ape could get her.

She didn't even know if she could sneak out and rush around the other side of the house. This way, she might be able to circle around and get to Craig after the brute had finished doing whatever he was doing. Then at least there was a chance that she could—

In the middle of her thoughts, a sudden creaking sound echoed down the hall, from the kitchen.

The skinny one was creeping into the library...

Biting her lower lip, Bobbie slipped quietly out into the hall. Trembling with fear, she swallowed a thick, wet lump in her throat and tiptoed quickly up the staircase.

***

Using the small pocket flashlight Ice had given him, Jett checked the library. Finding nothing, he went back out into the hall.

There was no sign of Ice at the screen door.

Alarmed, Jett hurried down the hall and peered outside through the screen. The big man was standing in the grass. The other guy was lying on his side, his back against the short brick wall, where flowers and plants lay dead in the dirt.

Ice pulled the revolver from his waistband, bent and spun the revolver around in his hand. The man on the ground tried twisting free. Ice stood about three feet behind him, watching curiously. The man jerked to his side and tried lashing out with his taped feet. Ice moved out of the way. When the man's heels slammed to the ground, Ice brought the gun down smartly on the back of the poor guy's head. The man arched his back, then went limp and lay still.

Before Jett could turn around and continue his investigation, Ice appeared around the corner. "Find anything yet?"

"Uh, no, Ice. I was just—"

"What're ya doin' here, then?"

"I was wonderin' what you were doin'. How'd ya know he was tryin' to get loose?"

"Heard him movin' around. C'mon." Ice gestured. "Let's go back inside. It shouldn't take us more than half an hour, tops, to check that damn house."

Chapter 8 - 9:15 P.M.

Upstairs, the overwhelming darkness engulfing Bobbie sent a crippling fear climbing up her spine.

Fumbling about, she whacked her right knee and left elbow on a doorway and a protruding doorknob. Knowing what would happen if she made a sound, she clenched her jaw to ward off the pain and gripped her handbag even tighter so she wouldn't drop it. If the two downstairs didn't hear anything, they might think no one else was in the house. She was reasonably certain neither of them had seen her, and she was determined to keep it that way.

There was no need to waste any more time analyzing this frightening situation. All that mattered was that two men had snuck of the bushes, knocked Craig unconscious, and taped him helpless. This was all she needed to convince her that her life was in extreme danger.

Using the penlight she kept in her handbag, she spotted an attic opening in the closet of the bedroom. Moving closer, she discovered that it was a white rectangular opening, about one-and-a-half by two-and-a-half feet, built into the ceiling of the small closet. Three wall shelves around two feet deep led up to it. If she could climb them, she might be able to push the trap open and crawl up. She could probably hide there safely until the two men searched the house and decided to leave.

It suddenly occurred to her that if she could find it, so could they. But since it was her only means of escape, she didn't have the time to explore any other option.

A light bulb hung from a ceiling fixture about three feet from the attic opening. Once she eased the door closed, she pulled the chain and spent the next twenty seconds memorizing the layout of the shelves. She pulled the chain again to turn off the light. Then, clamping the penlight between her teeth, she stood on the bottom shelf and unscrewed the bulb. She dropped it in her shoulder bag and hoisted it and her jacket onto the top shelf. Then she heaved herself up by springing off the bottom shelf. It gave a little, but she didn't think her hundred and fifteen pounds would cause it to collapse. Taking a deep breath, she pushed herself up, until her midsection pressed against the hard edge of the top shelf. With a final heave, she pulled herself onto the shelf, lifted a leg and rolled on over.

She lay on her back, staring at the attic paneling. She really had no choice, or the luxury of taking her time to consider other options. After a few quick breaths to gather her strength, she pressed both palms against the piece of plywood. Holding her breath, she gave it a tentative shove.

It didn't budge.

Her pulse raced. When was the last time someone used this stupid thing?

This wasn't the time to give up. Without hesitation, she raised her knees and brought them up to her chest. Then she raised her feet so the toes of her tennis shoes rested against the plywood trap.

Taking a deep breath, she applied a little more pressure and felt it give.

OPEN!

Shifting her legs, she positioned her toes more firmly against the wood. This time, the panel slid open further with a sharp crack. She shifted her legs again, toward the portion that had moved, and heaved all the way, until the trap opened another foot and stayed there, wedged tightly against its wooden borders, strands of cobwebs dangling near the opening.

Propping herself up on an elbow and using the penlight, she investigated the opening.

Was it big enough for her to slip through? And could she get it closed again without making enough racket to wake the dead?

Vibrations were coming from downstairs, directly beneath her.

Her heart flipped; she felt as if she'd just crawled out of a dropped elevator. For several incredibly long, agonizing moments, she lay absolutely still and just listened.

Someone was running up the stairs.

***

Once Ice had switched on the lights to the second floor, Jett ran up the stairs and reached the upper landing in a flash.

For the next five minutes he opened doors, checked underneath beds, and peeked inside closets. He checked the rooms on the right side of the stairs first. He figured that since they were darkest, they'd serve as good hiding places.

He found six rooms on the second floor—four bedrooms, a spare room, and one bath. When he'd finished checking one side of the house, he hurried back out into the hall and did the same on the other side of the house.

A few minutes later, he snuck into what looked like the largest bedroom and froze.

He was certain that he'd heard something coming from that room.

Chapter 9 - 9:30 P.M.

Trembling, Bobbie realized at once that she'd done something that could cause her horrible death.

Seconds earlier, she'd managed to close the small plywood opening by putting her weight on it. To her horror, the panel creaked as it lowered an inch or two before suddenly slamming shut with a muffled thump—a sound she was certain could be heard downstairs.

For long, agonizing minutes she sat completely still, her heart racing, her limbs trembling. She expected to hear them running up the stairs and rushing into the room.

After hearing only silence, she realized she might have been imagining things. They might have been making enough racket themselves to cover any minor noise she made. Hopefully she wasn't just being overly optimistic. After all, if they *had* heard something, she would have already heard them coming long before now.

She listened for another full minute. Then, still hearing nothing, she aimed her penlight above her head. A light hung down just a few feet from the paneled opening. A bulb was screwed into a white porcelain sconce drilled into the wooden rafter. She grasped the short copper chain dangling from it and pulled.

The area was instantly enveloped in a yellow haze.

Somewhat relieved, Bobbie pocketed her penlight and surveyed her surroundings.

Plywood ran in long sheets for about twenty feet, toward what was probably the upstairs hall. The plywood was raised about twenty feet from her position. The hall ceiling was obviously higher than the bedroom ceiling. It wouldn't be difficult to crawl on over to investigate. A house this size might have an escape route through another bedroom.

Thick, rectangular wads of insulation wedged between the rafters had yellowed with age and dampness from the elements. Additional chunks covered in foil were sandwiched between the two-by-fours of the attic floor. Since there were no windows, she couldn't be seen from outside. On the minus side, she wouldn't be able to escape through the roof.

Hazy shapes cluttered the passageway. Craig had told her his agent hired someone to clean up the place. She guessed that whoever he'd hired wouldn't have bothered to tidy up the attic. This could be a stroke of luck. You never could tell what you'd find in the attic of an old farmhouse.

She set down her bag gently on the plywood sheeting. She decided that the safest place she could be right now was sitting on the attic panel. She didn't think anyone could push it open while she was sitting on it. Unless, of course, whoever doing it possessed superhuman strength.

With a sigh, she fell on her side and lay still, trying to recover some of her strength. She strongly suspected she'd soon need every bit of it.

Moments later, she felt shaking.

Someone was entering the bedroom.

***

Jett checked under the bed but found nothing.

He straightened, crossed the room, and opened the closet door.

The closet was empty.

He turned back to the bed. It showed no activity and looked neat. Someone had obviously fixed it recently.

He began wondering about that thumping noise he'd just heard.

Was it the lady Ice thought had come here with the man?

If so, where was she hiding?

***

Ice came right in and scanned the room. "Bed looks too damn neat." He turned to Jett. "Any sign of a chick?"

Jett shrugged. "Checked everywhere, Ice. No sign of anyone."

Ice went over to the night table. There was nothing on it but an old lamp. "I just checked the kitchen. A bottle of wine on the sink counter, about three-quarters killed. There were two glasses, both empty."

"Maybe there *was* a lady here, Ice…"

He shook his head. "No lipstick on either glass. I just can't imagine a city chick not wearing war paint, especially when she comes out here to mess up the bed sheets with the boss. For him, she'd have to be perfect. And with a city chick, perfect means full makeup. These chicks can't go a damn hour without fixing their face, and the lipstick always gets top priority."

"What's it mean, then?"

"She ain't here, dammit. Mr. Big Shot mighta used both glasses. Maybe she was s'posed to meet him later on. Maybe she took too long, so he got tired of waitin' and decided to get buzzed on that shit." He went silent. Something was nagging at him—something he hadn't thought of before. "Didn't it look like the fucker was waitin' for somebody outside, on the front porch?"

"I dunno, Ice. I couldn't see from where I was."

"Maybe she's on her way out here as we speak." Ice went over to the bed. There was one sure way of checking out recent activity on a mattress. He grabbed a corner of the sheet and yanked the covers down, exposing the aged, sagging mattress underneath. He began sniffing, his nose just above the mattress.

Jett walked over. "Whatcha doin', Ice?"

Ice straightened. He knew full well what sex smelled like, but it just wasn't doing it for him right now. However, he also knew there could be other factors involved, throwing him off. "*Coulda* been a broad in this bed...but all I smell is mildew." He produced his cigarettes and got one going. "We'll wait for Mr. Big Shot to wake up. Then I'll flat-out ask him if she came with him. I already checked the Porsche to see if she left her bag, or a jacket or anything else in there, but I didn't see nothin'. If she's comin' later, we'll hide and wait. I'll leave the Porsche where it is and keep the truck in the bushes so she don't think somethin's up."

Jett didn't reply.

"In the meantime, we'll check around. If she's hidin, it's gotta be outside somewhere—some place we didn't check. We might as well try the barn and the other outbuildings while we're at it." He scratched the back of his neck. "Mighta found a place we didn't think of."

He reached into his side pocket and pulled out a wad of bills. "By the way, I found this in the man's pockets. Eight hundred smackers. He had six in his pocket."

Jett's eyes lit up. "We keepin' it, Ice?"

"Damn straight. Five-oh, five-oh. Three C-notes apiece. The man won't be needin' cash anymore. I left the other two in his wallet just in case the fire-boys get here super quick, and the cops wonder why he didn't have any cash on him."

"What's his name, Ice?"

Ice frowned. "Why?"

Jett shrugged. "Just thought we oughta know his name."

"Don't let it worry ya, kid. This is just a business transaction. It don't matter what Mr. Big Shot's name is—get it?"

"Got it, Ice."

Ice puffed thoughtfully on his cigarette. The kid needed to toughen up if he wanted to make his mark in this business. It was up to Ice to steer him in the right direction. To be successful in this business, you didn't want to humanize your mark. "We'll check the house again. I'll keep an eye on Mr. Big Shot and ask him about the babe when he comes to. Otherwise, we'll have to wait till morning. The Man told me she'll probably be here with her boss, but I learned a long time ago not to trust anything anyone tells me."

Jett nodded dutifully.

"If she's out here, she can't get far in the dark. Closest neighbor's more than six miles down that road. Some farm I saw when I was checkin' out the area." Ice dropped his spent smoke onto the floor and squished it with his boot. He went over to the closet. He put his weight on the bottom shelf, holding on to the top one while pushing on what looked like the trapdoor of an attic. The bottom shelf squealed loudly beneath the big man's weight. Ice gave the panel a shove. It didn't budge. The bottom shelf squealed a little more, bowing on its hinges.

Ice tried pushing the attic panel again. "Damn thing hasn't been touched in years. No way a chick could climb on up and open this damn thing when I can't even budge it."

With one last protest from the bottom shelf, Ice dropped down with a heavy thud. The shelf creaked a couple of times and sagged—clearly just a nudge or two short of tearing loose from its hinges.

"No way anyone opened that damn thing and crawled up there," he said.

Chapter 10 - 9:45 P.M.

Shivering in the darkness of the attic, Bobbie began breathing again.

She told herself not to move until she could no longer hear their muffled voices coming from below.

Only moments ago, she'd had horrifying visions of the big one marching into the closet, spotting the trap, reaching up and forcing his fist through it…or taking out his gun and shooting at it. She imagined herself crashing through the jagged strips and falling to the floor below, at their feet.

Then, during her nightmare fantasy, she'd heard someone in the closet. Her pulse pounded heavily in her ears. Her head seemed encased in a glass bowl, magnifying each noise. She had to cover her mouth with both hands to prevent the scream from tearing out of her throat.

Would they think she'd climbed up here?

Would they replace the missing light bulb?

Her heart suddenly shot right up her throat when she felt the slight nudge on the underside of the plywood just two inches from her butt.

My God! He's coming up!

A moment later, a loud crash made the walls vibrate.

It sounded like someone had fallen to the floor directly below her.

Then she heard muffled voices. Since they were speaking softly, she couldn't make out what they were saying.

But it didn't matter what they were saying. To hear them better, she'd have to shift her position and press her ear to the plywood. To do that, she'd probably give her position away.

She refused to move an inch. In fact, she wouldn't move at all. She didn't think she'd ever be able to move again...

Minutes later, she heard only silence. After waiting another minute or so, she no longer heard anything, and told herself it was okay to breathe again. She began with slow, even breaths, and was extra careful that she made no sound. When her heart finally continued functioning again, she began to rationalize.

Were they criminals? Escapees from the Federal pen in Moundsville?

It could explain how they'd appeared out of nowhere. They'd obviously stolen a vehicle, driven here to get away and decided to use the woods for seclusion. They might have been looking for some place to stay and hide out when they saw the lights coming from the house. They could have been admiring the isolation of the place when they spotted Craig and decided that if they wanted to use the house, he had to be taken out of the picture...

My dear God....

Convicts, of all people...

They probably haven't been with a woman in years!

73

She fought down the cold panic and forced herself to think rationally. However, she just couldn't stop the terrifying images from filling her mind.

74

Chapter 11 - 10:00 P.M.

Ice approached the top of the staircase and stopped.

"Somethin's buggin' me." He looked up at the faded wooden panel ceiling directly above his head, where an attic staircase had been fitted in its center.

"Think she went up there to hide?" Jett asked.

Ice frowned. "You see a *chain* hangin' down from it?"

"Nope..."

"Then how the hell would she be able to get up there?"

"Dunno, Ice."

Ice studied the rectangular wooden panel. The closest light, the fixture over the head of the stairs, blazed more than ten feet away. How the hell could anyone yank the damned thing open?

It might be just a replacement panel in the ceiling. The elements, over the years, may have rotted some of the roof, causing leakage. If it was actually an attic staircase, a chain would be hanging down from the edge of the panel. The ceiling was a good ten feet up—there was no way anyone could jump up, pull the panel open, climb the stairs and pull it closed.

If a female *was* hiding in the house, she had to be somewhere else. But if they came up empty, he'd want to have a look up there, just to make sure.

"Let's check the rest of the house. When we're finished, we'll take a little trip outside and bring in

Mr. Big Shot. Then we might as well get some shuteye. Tomorrow, I gotta phone The Man at twelve noon and tell him everything's A-okay. But if that bitch is anywhere on this property, we need to find her. There's entirely too much money involved to risk with this gig."

***

Bobbie pulled the light chain and held her breath.

She'd expected to hear yelling, to feel someone pounding on the panel beneath her. When the heavy silence continued, she resumed breathing. Just then, she felt light-headed and rubbed her temples. It sure was warm up here. She squirmed carefully out of her lightweight denim jacket and opened her bag. After removing the light bulb she'd unscrewed from the closet, she found her penknife and shoved it in her jeans. Then she stuffed the jacket in her bag.

Moments later, she realized how thirsty she was.

Stop it. Concentrate on getting out of this alive. Then *you can start thinking about indulging yourself...*

There seemed to be enough room up here to move about freely, without knocking into things. Farther down, in the raised section, the area was cluttered with boxes. There could be an assortment of kitchen knives or other useful weapons lying amongst the clutter.

Even so, she had to face reality. Her scope of investigation was severely limited. She could hardly hunt through those boxes without making noise. It would be impossible to discover anything useful without alerting them of her presence.

She just hoped they wouldn't try the attic panel again…

***

Ice flicked on all the lights in the house.

For the next two hours, he thoroughly checked every nook and cranny big enough to hide the average-sized female.

The living room didn't take long at all. It was a large room, with an old couch and a couple of armchairs arranged in the center, a block fireplace at the far end, oak cabinets built into the front wall and a bookcase covering the opposite wall. After checking out the bookcase cabinets, he tried the fireplace.

The world's smallest midget couldn't squeeze through the six-inch-gap at the opening, which served as the flue. It would be no problem, blocking the flue when the time came. He'd dump a load of wood in there, fire her up good with newspapers then knock over the rusty old fire-screen so the flames could jump onto the throw-rug. One of the battered armchairs sat about six feet away. He pushed it a little closer.

He crossed the room and went through the archway into the next room. An old dinette set sat in the center area, with a corner hutch and an antique china cabinet dominating the opposite wall. He checked the cabinet drawers but found nothing.

The next stop was the kitchen. He and Jett had checked it before, but since he didn't want to leave anything to chance, he checked again. For all they

77

knew, she could have doubled back when they were upstairs.

The cabinets took no time at all. They were empty.

The tiny powder room at the far end of the kitchen was next on the agenda. He found no lingering perfume scents or forgotten items belonging to a female.

Beyond the kitchen, the narrow room sat, empty except for an old table and chairs.

Disappointed, he went over to the kitchen sink and gazed out the bay window. A cigarette dangled from his mouth; a scowl dominated his lined features.

If that broad had come here, where the hell was she?

He'd find out what was going on when Mr. Big Shot woke up.

***

Moving as cautiously and as silently as a cat, Bobbie crawled along the plywood floor of the attic.

The area farther down would provide a much larger workspace. She crawled over to one wall and found a gray metal toolbox in one of the boxes sitting amongst the clutter. She gingerly went through its contents, placing things gently on the plywood sheeting beside her.

She found a long-shafted, regular-headed screwdriver, an ancient penknife with a cracked plastic handle and three dull, rusty working blades, two rusted blades from an old circular saw, a nail punch and a short crowbar about two feet long.

78

For now, her plan was to carve a small slit in the floorboards directly above the attic stairs. It was crucial to fashion some sort of crude observation point to monitor the activity below her so she could have an idea of what they were doing and where they were.

She crawled over to the staircase contraption and inspected the boards. There was no plywood covering the two-by-fours around it, so carving a peephole would be fairly simple. She decided to use her own knife. It was much sharper, larger and easier to hold than the one she'd found in the toolbox. Using short scratching movements with the blade and carefully blowing away the scrapings to prevent them from falling through the boards and accumulating on the bare wooden floor downstairs, she'd be able to create a small but effective peephole.

It would take some time, but there was nothing else she could do. She needed to keep a constant watch on them and monitor their movements if she wanted to get out of this mess.

What did she have to lose?

Chapter 12 - 12:00 A.M.

Ice went out back with his pocket flashlight and began checking the rear of the house.

Normally, there were only so many places a body could hide. But at night? In the dark?

It was even worse out here, with trees and hills blending in with the darkness.

If Sheffield's bitch *was* out here, Ice had to find her as quickly as possible. The difficult part would be getting her taped up without hurting her. There couldn't be any marks on her when he and Jett put her in the house with Sheffield. He could probably just point the gun at her and convince her he meant business—that her only hope was to cooperate.

Chicks were usually terrified of guns.

This seemed simple in theory, but Ice frequently had problems handling women. His hormones had the nasty habit of taking over. He'd already explained this to the Man, but it didn't seem to matter. The asshole seemed genuinely interested when he discovered how Ice could lose his cool in the heat of the situation. Ice couldn't shake the feeling that the Man *wanted* him to make the woman suffer.

Using his flashlight, Ice went back up the hill. If he did find her, he promised himself a piece of her first. He'd have to tie her down first, but that came with the territory. Anyway, it seemed to get his rocks off easier. Afterward, he'd smother her right beside her boyfriend, and that would be that.

His thoughts immediately shifted to the Spanish whore he'd hooked up with two months earlier. As always, he felt his juices heating up when he thought about it. Two months was just too damn long to go without a quality piece of ass. His hormones needed release way more often than that.

Daytona Beach might be just the thing to relieve all this stress.

Even so, he couldn't stop thinking of that wild spic. She was one of those loud, arrogant females that wanted to run the show. But once he got her stripped and tied down, she'd turned out just fine.

Ice switched off the flashlight and moved quietly up the winding dirt path. He had no problem feeling his way in the dark.

He *liked* feeling his way.

It sharpened the senses.

***

After nearly half an hour, Bobbie managed to create a small slit in the attic floor half an inch long and just deep enough between the boards to permit her to see the faintest haze on the landing below. She scraped the wood carefully with the short blade of the knife, back and forth, blowing frequently to nudge the shavings out of her work area.

An urge had been growing in her as she labored, but she shoved it in the back of her mind. She hoped this concern would blend in with the rest of the clutter, enabling her to concentrate fully on what she was doing. It was that last cup of coffee she'd had at the office before meeting Craig in the parking garage. She'd only had half a cup, but even so, it had been enough to make its presence known in her bladder.

Darn. She didn't even like that brand of coffee—especially the stuff the guys at the office drank. It tasted like vanilla-flavored battery acid most of the time. If only she'd put the cup back down the moment she poured it... If only Craig had gotten out of his stupid meeting an hour earlier... If only she'd had the intestinal fortitude to tell him she had other things to do, and couldn't come with him on this mindless last-minute excursion...

Stop whining. Finish working on your peephole. Then you can find some way of relieving yourself.

Forcing her mind back on the task at hand, she tried her best to ignore her full bladder.

Back-and-forth, back-and-forth, scrape, blow...
***

Using Ice's pocket flashlight, Jett checked out the basement.

The area had a low beamed ceiling and was separated into four sections. The room facing the far wall had probably once been a damp, sour-smelling fruit cellar. There was no door, and the top of the doorway barely cleared Jett's five feet, six inches. The moment he stepped through the doorway, the heavy cobwebs forming a wavy chain-link fence extending from the ceiling to the sloped stone floor made him stop abruptly and back up. Anyone hiding in there would have disturbed those cobwebs.

A soot-covered, cast-iron coal furnace occupied most of the central area. Someone had fashioned a small workshop area with homemade shelves and a long wooden bench underneath the stairs. Dusty jars half-filled with rusty nails and carpet tacks hung from a shelf. A paint-smeared putty knife lay on a different shelf, the coated edge sticking out. A battered toolbox, its lid open, provided the perfect home for dust-covered screwdrivers and crescent wrenches. Half a dozen cans of paint, their sides caked with hardened strings and bubbles of every conceivable color, took up additional space on the worktable.

A wooden stepladder hung from two L-shaped aluminum hooks drilled into the cracked concrete wall. A couple of rusty canning lids with BB dents in their centers lay on the uneven concrete floor.

The remaining area had been used for storage. Jett went over to the foul-smelling area, where boxes and crates filled with junk were stacked to the rotted beams in the ceiling.

"Lady?" Jett kept his voice soft and friendly. If she'd come down here, he could convince her he meant no harm. He had the roll of tape in his back pocket and could get her taped up in no time if he could distract her properly. He could talk real sweet and get her to show herself. Ladies liked it when you talked sweet to them. It made them feel special. Momma had melted when her boyfriends pulled the sweet bit even after they'd slapped her around.

If this lady was hiding down here, she couldn't know what they'd done with her boyfriend. He could've just left, for all she knew. Gone somewhere else and left her here, all alone.

"Lady? Ya down here?" He snuck over to the furnace and checked to see if the big metal latch had been moved. He felt around, listening for sounds. It didn't seem to be hooked up.

Would a lady hide in a furnace in a strange place at night?

He tried peering through the soot-covered vents, but it was too dark and clogged with gunk to make out anything.

"Lady, if you're down here, why don'tcha just come on out? We ain't gonna hurt ya none. Ice and me, we came out here to...to do a job for your boyfriend."

That was good, he thought. *It came right on out, slicker than greased owl shit*. Ice would be pleased.

"Yeah, we're gonna be workin' for him...and we came here to talk about the job." He snuck over to the coal bin and pointed the light beam straight ahead. He had a look at its wooden door, which had rotted clean through and hung lopsided by its rusty hinges.

"We're s'posed to do some work on the barn." He smiled at that last statement, knowing how much smarter he was getting since he'd teamed up with Ice. "Me and Ice, we're carpenters. Every now and then we let folks know we're lookin' for some extra work."

Jett pointed the light behind two beat-up, crud covered old Maytags. Cracked, peeling coils of black hose had been shoved against the concrete wall. Cobwebs dangled everywhere, looping here and there, extending loosely from one dusty foothold to the next.

84

"That's what we were doin' before we came inside. Ice and your boyfriend, they're out back, checkin' out the barn…"

He suddenly stopped talking.

Someone was upstairs, moving about.

***

After several more minutes of furious scraping, Bobbie's peephole permitted her to glimpse the upstairs hall, the top of the stairs and a portion of the bedroom doorway to the right.

By this time, her bladder was ready to burst. It was all she could do to keep from wetting herself as she continued rubbing away at the crack between the boards. She forced herself to concentrate on the job, believing her bladder was really empty, that it was becoming a nuisance because she hadn't put anything in it for a while.

She *was* thirsty but had kept that in the back of her mind with the rest of this nightmare. Otherwise, she knew she wouldn't be able to concentrate on the peephole.

When she blew away the last of the wood shavings to reveal the welcomed glare of the hall lighting, the relief she felt for this major accomplishment caused her urge to subside, if only for a moment.

The first thing she did was make sure her pocket penlight was always close. Because of the opening she'd created, it was now necessary to switch off the overhead light bulb. Even a miniscule glint through the boards could be seen if someone was looking up.

85

She rummaged through her bag, pulled a cotton ball from her makeup kit, and put it near her peephole. When she wasn't using it, she'd use the cotton to plug it up.

She flicked off the light bulb, got down on her stomach and kept her eyes and ears open. When the pain in her hips and elbows proved too much, she sat up and massaged her cramping muscles and joints. While she recovered, she thought over what she'd observed.

There was no sign of anyone, and no sound of any kind.

Had the two men given up? Had they been frightened off?

Or had they just gotten bored and fled?

She got back down on her stomach and watched through the peephole.

No sign of life.

This was plain silly. Why should she stay up here until she starved to death, playing hide-and-seek with two men who were probably gone by now? It made absolutely no sense to hide in an attic, waiting for two men who were no longer there to climb up after her.

She waited a few more minutes, and as her bladder pounded its urgent message, it became even clearer to her that she should leave the attic. She began thinking of the bathroom. It sat at the end of the hall, just twenty or thirty feet away. It would take less than a minute to make it there once she'd left the attic.

The thought of relieving herself suddenly became the most important thing in her life.

Once she'd taken care of that, she could rush down the steps, find Craig and try and revive him. Then, if those two hadn't taken his cell phone, she could get someone out here, tell them what happened and get them to take her and Craig back to Wheeling.

She pushed herself back up and turned on her penlight. With a deep breath, she turned and prepared herself for the crawl back to the attic panel.

An instant later, she froze.

The slamming of the screen door downstairs made her heart skip a beat.

Chapter 13 - 12:45 A.M.

After checking Mr. Big Shot's pulse, Ice went back inside and met Jett out in the hall, near the door that led to the basement stairs. "Find anything?"

"Nope. Looked everywhere, too. Think she's on her way out here, Ice?"

"Maybe." Ice went into the kitchen and opened the refrigerator door. A bottle of wine and two bags of food from one of those fancy Wheeling restaurants sat on the middle shelf. He checked the bags. Three plastic containers—one of shrimp salad and the other two with that vinegary pasta shit he hated. It was kind of obvious that Mr. Big Shot was planning on a cozy little shindig. "There's enough food here for a day or two. Reminds me. Go out to the truck and bring in the Wild Turkey. I'm gonna need more whiskey if we have to stay here any longer."

"How long ya think we'll be here, Ice?"

"Just long enough to find out what's goin' on. I'll need some time to get the fire goin'. We can't finish this deal till then. I gotta make the call in less than twelve hours, then get the fire goin' by dinnertime. Might as well make the best of it till then."

"What about the lady?"

"Whaddya mean?"

Jett shrugged. "I mean, if we find her—"

88

"We do the job, whether we find her or not. Whaddya *think* is gonna happen?"

Jett fidgeted. "I just thought…"

"Ya thought what?"

Jett reddened.

Ice snorted laughter. "*You* wanna crack at her? Go right ahead. Five-oh, five-oh—right down the wire. Remember?"

Jett laughed nervously.

Ice shook his head. It was a damn shame the kid's momma messed up her baby boy so bad. A grown man twenty-two years old, and he never had a real piece of ass… It was damn pitiful.

"Get the whiskey." He patted Jett between the shoulder blades and thought of Lonnie once again. Then he forced himself to focus. "I'll get Mr. Big Shot and haul him inside, before a coon or wild dog makes off with him. I'll take him upstairs so he's out of the way in case his girlfriend shows up later on."

Jett nodded.

"Bastard don't come to soon, I'll have to help him along."

"Why's he been out so long, Ice?"

"I probably just whacked him too hard."

"Think you can wake him up?"

"I got my ways. Now go get the whiskey."

Jett hurried out of the room.

Ice grabbed the flashlight and thought about Mr. Big Shot's chick again. If she was coming to meet the bastard, she should've been here already. It was almost one in the morning.

On his way down the hall, Ice stopped at the foot of the stairs and glanced upwards. He'd soon have a good long look at that attic. Right now, he was just too damned tired.

Gettin' old, he reminded himself. *Old joints just don't bounce back like they did five, ten years ago.*

Such thoughts made him want to do two or three more hits, then retire. Maybe in Rio, where the babes did every square inch of you for a ten-spot.

Ice turned back to the job at hand and thought about the attic opening in the bedroom closet. Then he considered getting his crowbar to pry the damned thing open.

***

When the voices downstairs died down, Bobbie sat up to rest her tense joints and massage her aching neck.

She wanted to scream but knew she couldn't. It was best to stay focused and continue thinking of ways to survive.

Making sure her cotton swab plugged her peephole, she turned on the overhead light and thought of her next plan of action.

Her main priority, of course, was her overwhelming urge to pee.

Very carefully she crawled over to where the boxes were stacked. She went through a box, once again placing everything gently on the plywood floor beside her. To her delight, she found half a dozen empty Mason quart jars, their rubber-lined lids bunched loosely in a crumpled old paper bag. She placed two of the jars carefully on the plywood floor. She didn't think she'd need both but didn't know how long she'd be up here. She didn't even want to entertain the possibility that she might have to stay here for days…

Forcing herself to focus on the important issue, she reached for her bag, opened it, pulled out her jacket and checked the bag. The thick wad of Kleenex she carried for emergencies immediately caught her eye. She gingerly peeled down the designer jeans. Cursing herself for wearing them so tight, she pushed down the sheer pink panties until they cleared her knees. She spread her thighs and squatted, lowering herself until she was positioned above the four-inch opening of the jar.

The area immediately grew thick with the heavy ammoniac smell.

Once she'd finished, she dropped the damp Kleenex in the jar. She screwed the lid on, straightened and hiked up her panties and jeans. After buckling her belt, she picked up the jar.

She found a suitable hiding place between two boxes jammed against the back wall. She wedged the jar in there, took the empty and put it in a safe but convenient place.

Relieved, she returned to her peephole. After lowering herself carefully into lookout position, she reached up, switched off the light and pulled out the cotton swab. The instant she lowered her right eye directly over the hole, she felt something cold crawling up her spine.

The skinny one was looking up at her from the bottom of the stairs.

***

Jett was certain he'd heard a strange noise.

91

He stood just a few feet from the bottom step of the staircase, whiskey bottle in hand, gazing up at the top of the stairs.

It sounded like a loud creak, then a soft, distant thump.

He reminded himself that this was an old house, and everyone knew old houses were known for creaks and thumps and other scary things. He remembered strange noises that happened in an old house in the middle of the night, when he was a small boy.

He and Momma had lived in some scary places when he was younger, places they'd had to live in when Momma was out making money. Jett was left home alone many times. The only times he wasn't left alone were when one of Momma's girlfriends came over to watch him when they weren't working.

He'd spent many a night in unfamiliar places, shivering in the dark, his covers pulled up all the way, his pillow pulled over his head so he couldn't hear the monsters whispering. When he didn't hear the monsters, he heard giggling coming from another room...or the wind whistling through the cracks in the windowpane.

However, strange noises were strange noises. He was already jumpy enough.

He began wondering if he'd heard rats.

When he was ten, he and Momma had found a dead rat in the closet in the brick house in downtown Bridgeport. The damned thing had been half the size of a cat and had eaten some of the tiling before crawling into the woodwork to die.

Momma's girlfriend, Fay, had been staying with them at the time. Fay was called "Daisy Fay" because she was always taking daisies from the front yard and putting them in a glass vase she'd fashioned from an old peanut butter jar, which she kept on the windowsill.

Fay's golden-brown hair always glittered in the light after she'd washed and brushed it. Fay was tall and lean, and her long, slender limbs flowed when she walked. Fay worked with Momma for a while and spent many a night on the living room couch when her old man kicked her out. Fay sang to Jett when Momma was out, working. She even gave him a special treat the day he'd turned sixteen.

Fay had crept silently into the room, bent over his bed, and gave him a whiskey-drenched kiss before pulling his covers down. She hadn't said anything, just slid down his undershorts and made him feel really good.

Jett wondered if Mr. Big Shot's lady would make him feel as good. Probably not, since she'd probably have to be tied down, and wouldn't feel very sociable.

Jett suddenly smiled. It wouldn't be all *that* bad, would it? A chick tied down and helpless? The image made him feel hot and tense. It also made him forget about the noise he'd just heard.

"What the hell ya doin', standin' there like an idiot?"

Jett spun around. Ice was standing in the doorway. Still taped up, Mr. Big Shot was draped over the big man's massive right shoulder.

Jett wanted to tell Ice something important but, for some reason, couldn't remember what it was. It had seemed important at the time, but somehow he just couldn't remember it right now. "Nothin', Ice. I just thought—"

"Never mind. Just get outa my way. This fucker's gettin' heavy."

"Where ya takin' him?"

"Upstairs. When I want answers, it'll be easier stakin' him out to work him over. If the broad shows, he'll be out of sight when she comes in."

"Whatcha want me to do now, Ice?"

"Take good care of that whiskey. I'll be right back down for it."

***

Someone was trudging up the stairs.

Bobbie immediately froze. It felt like a hot coal had just dropped in her gut. Luckily, she hadn't put much weight on the plywood. Otherwise, whoever was coming up would have surely heard the creaking noise.

The footfalls were very heavy, making the walls vibrate. The one ascending the stairs was no doubt the massive brute she'd seen through the window. He was the one holding the gun on Craig. He also looked like he really enjoyed hurting people.

The footfalls continued.

Her heart thundering like a jackhammer, she forced herself not to move, or even breathe. She didn't want him even thinking about the attic.

Sudden silence.

What was he doing? Looking around? Or just listening?

Bobbie froze and held her breath.

Moments later, the footfalls resumed.

More silence.

She stayed on her side on the plywood sheeting and forced herself to remain in this position. She knew it would be stupid to move around. She didn't even attempt to look at her peephole. That would require movement—a change of position. She knew better than that.

Anyway, she didn't see any need to look right now. The only thing that made any sense was to remain completely still and hope that the big brute didn't have any reason to suspect someone was directly overhead.

***

Ice dumped Mr. Big Shot on the big double bed and stood beside the bed, watching him.

The man lay on his back on the mattress, ankles taped together, and wrists taped behind his back with the fresh strip Ice had yanked from the roll to replace what the fucker had damaged earlier.

After about a minute, Ice held his palm close to the man's nostrils.

Warm air came out in thin trickles.

Straightening, Ice glanced at his watch and wondered how long the man would stay unconscious. Their timetable didn't allow for all this wasted effort.

He suddenly wondered if the bastard was playing possum.

There was one sure way to find out.

Ice reached down and jammed the first two fingers of his right hand into the man's unprotected crotch.

Mr. Big Shot merely turned his head slightly on the pillow.

Ice scratched his brush cut. When a dude received a serious jab to the balls, he automatically forgot everything else and yelled loud enough to wake the dead. No, this bastard was definitely out cold.

Ice rubbed his temples. He was getting tired and thirsty. The thought of the Wild Turkey bottle waiting for him in the kitchen made this session kind of pointless.

"You lucked out, asshole. This time, anyway." Then he turned and left the room.

***

Bobbie pressed her ear to the wooden floor but heard nothing.

The silence nipped at her, and she wondered what happened.

Was he still on the floor below? It made her wonder why he'd come upstairs in the first place.

Was he checking the rooms again?

She lay completely still, this time with one eye directly over the peephole. Before she realized it, sheer exhaustion had swept in. It had come from out of nowhere, overpowering her and surrounding her in a soft gray cloud.

Long before she realized it, she'd drifted off.

PART TWO

THE HUNTER

Chapter 14 - 5:30 A.M.

Ice woke up on the living room floor.

He and Jett had taken the cushions from the battered old couch and fashioned them into beds in the corner, which was darker than the rest of the room and hidden from view from the hall. It would give them the best advantage if Sheffield's girlfriend showed. The living room was lit by the hall light; anyone coming in would be drawn to that room, rather than the corner, which remained dark. Ice decided to leave the lights as Sheffield had fixed them just in case his girlfriend had chosen to show up early in the morning.

He sat up heavily. The cushion was thin and lumpy and hadn't afforded his lower back much comfort. After a little stretching to get the kinks out, he turned and squinted at the parted curtains. As the last remnants of sleep subsided, he saw that it was still dark outside. He yawned, adjusted his position, and rubbed his scalp. Then he grabbed his lightweight jacket from the floor and checked the pockets.

Everything was there: wallet, keys, money, change, knife. The revolver lay under the cushion, within easy reach. He didn't think the kid would roll him, but you just never knew. After all, the boy had grown up with hookers.

Ice had been out of lockup more than five years but still slept with one eye open. Sleeping light was necessary for survival. You slept a few minutes at a time, your shiv in your fist under your pillow, your senses alert. If you were lucky, they stuck you with a cellmate you could kick around so you didn't have to worry about him shivving you in the middle of the night for cigarettes or coke money. If not, you did him in and took your chances in Solitary.

Luckily, Ice didn't have to spend much time in prison. Fourteen hundred and ten days, all told. With the help of a Pennsylvania politician who'd wanted a rival offed quietly, that Ohio shyster had gotten him paroled early. Now he was out, doing what he wanted—nobody on his case, harassing him at all hours, opening his mail or checking his bunk.

Ice could tell no one had tried opening the front door. For one thing, his sensitive sleeping habits would have detected anyone on the porch. For another, the simple booby trap he'd rigged with fishing line would have alerted him even if he'd been in a drunken stupor. It was a good thing the kitchen door was boarded up.

The kid still hadn't moved. He lay on the other cushion, skinny arms and legs splayed out, his head cocked at an odd angle.

Ice thought once again about keeping Jett with him. The boy needed him. The little shit made him feel almost like a father...

Ice shook his head. The idea was almost laughable. The closest he'd ever come to that was ten, maybe twelve years ago, when he and Gina were first married. That false alarm had the two of them uneasy and irritable until they'd got the good news from her doctor.

It would never have worked. Gina had never been the motherly type. She'd always been too concerned about her figure, spending money and having a good time. Good thing she *hadn't* popped something out. The kid would've needed a *real* mother right off.

He unwound the fishing line from the fingers of his right hand. Then he got up and went into the hall to remove the slipknot from the doorstop. He pocketed the line, lit a cigarette, and plodded down the hall, to the kitchen. He pulled out a bag from the fridge, set it on the counter and kicked the door closed. When he opened the bag, he saw the same shit as before—shrimp salad with that fancy white sauce smeared all over it. Not bad for a day or so, but Ice craved something more substantial. Nothing hit the spot better than a twenty-four-ounce, blood-rare Porterhouse steak, baked potato smeared in butter and sour cream, and a pint of Wild Turkey.

The shrimp would have to do. The Wild Turkey was nearly shot. Just a few hours ago he'd chugged down a good three inches, waiting for the woman to show.

Focusing on more pressing matters, Ice unwrapped a dozen shrimp, put them on a napkin and stuck them in the microwave. The microwave was one of those small jobs you bought for an RV. Ol' Sheff probably picked it up when he started bringing his whores here.

99

Ice had a tiny sip of the Wild Turkey while the shrimp heated up. He decided to wait until the whiskey was gone before trying out that infernal wine. Crap tasted like recycled piss, but it would just have to do.

He was munching on some shrimp on his way back to the living room when the boy stirred.

"Where'd ya go, Ice?"

"Just checkin' things out." He went over to the window and looked out at the silver Porsche as he ate. He shook his head. Damn thing probably went for close to two hundred grand. Big shots were all alike. They all went after the same shit—top-of-the-line rides, imported suits, fancy-ass foods and wines, and the best-looking hookers. It was a damn shame big money was wasted on the wrong people.

The kid sat up, yawning. "Hungry," he said, his voice raspy.

Ice gestured to the doorway. "In the kitchen. There's a shitload of shrimp left, and that other stuff. It's better than nothin'. Get yourself somethin' to eat."

Jett heaved himself up into a standing position and crossed the room.

Chapter 15 - 6:15 A.M.

After finishing his disappointing breakfast, Ice went upstairs to check on Mr. Big Shot.

The man hadn't moved at all. Bubbles of slimy snot had come out of his nostrils, gathering on both cheeks and the tape covering his mouth.

Ice lowered his hand and checked the man's breathing.

He felt nothing.

Shit. I hit the fucker too damn hard.

He took a corner of the tape sealing the man's mouth and pulled. Foul-smelling upchuck bubbled out through Sheffield's parted lips, forming thick streams of syrupy goo sliding down his chin.

"*Dammit.*" Ice rolled Sheffield over on his side and pounded the man between the shoulder blades with the flat of his hand. More greenish gray upchuck sprayed outwards, collecting in small chunks on the faded bedspread.

"Great. Just fuckin' great." Ice let Sheffield roll onto his back. Then he composed himself and checked for a pulse in the man's neck and then listened closely for a heartbeat.

The man was dead, all right. He'd obviously choked to death.

Ice turned, crossed the room, and stood at the top of the stairs. "Jett!"

Nothing.

"Dammit, Jett! Get your ass out here!"

Seconds later, the kid appeared at the foot of the stairs. "What's up, Ice?"

Ice couldn't speak for several moments. The heat had swept through him, and he found that he couldn't think straight. Sheffield was dead—which meant they couldn't find out anything more about the woman unless they investigated for themselves. *Dammit...*

"Ice?" The kid was waiting.

Ice took a breath and tried to calm himself. They could do this. It would take a little longer, but they could do it. "Fucker's dead. He choked to death, drowned in his own vomit."

The kid put on one of his stupid expressions. Ice thought he was going to have to explain it better, but the boy finally nodded.

"Now we have to make damn sure we find this chick. If she's anywhere within a mile of this place, we gotta get her and bring her here." He descended the stairs heavily. "Too damn much money restin' on this to piss it all away."

***

Bobbie opened her eyes but saw only darkness.

She was lying on her stomach on something hard and uneven. Her right arm tingled as the numbness in her fingertips made her grind her teeth.

Voices had wrenched her from the darkness—back to a much darker, colder reality. Remembering instantly where she was, she turned gingerly on her side. Her arm continued tingling; she shook it. Working through the pain, she groped for her penlight, flicked it on and aimed it at her watch.

6:19. How long had she been asleep?

The urge overwhelming her right now was a glass of cool, clear water... A drink. She'd *kill* for a drink of fresh spring water...

Stop it. And focus.

She switched off the penlight and pulled the cotton from her peephole. Sleep had fogged up her eyes. She squeezed them shut and forced herself to wake up...to concentrate and focus.

Once her vision cleared, she went back to her peephole. Someone with a shaved head and huge shoulders was standing directly below her, at the top of the stairs.

It was the big brute...

"Fucker's dead. He choked to death, drowned in his own vomit."

Dead. Had she heard him right? Craig? Dead?

A solid ball of ice slid painfully down her spine, and her entire body tensed up.

My God my God my DEAR SWEET GOD!

Craig? Dead?

No. *NO!*

Dead. Drowned in his own vomit...

This was so...so *awful*...so *horrible*!

And all because he'd brought her here...

Now the man was dead because two killers had just murdered him. And they were probably still looking for her.

Then, during her terror, she heard the brute report the most frightening message of all: "Too damn much money restin' on this to piss it all away."

Money. This was all about money.

103

My God. These two had come here to kill Craig for money...

She struggled to keep the tears from rolling down her cheeks. Was this grief—this anguish—because of Craig? After all, she didn't really like the man, did she? He was her boss, but that didn't mean she actually *liked* him, did it? No. She *didn't* like him. She didn't like *any* man who cheated on his wife.

But that wasn't why she wanted to cry, was it? No. Now she was completely on her own, and there were two men downstairs who were going to kill her if they found her.

This had nothing to do with Craig and everything to do with her survival. She *had* to stay in control...to keep from giving up totally.

I can't scream...or hit anything...or pull out my hair... I have to go through this agony in total silence.

Her only option, of course, was to hold the terror in—to keep it hidden deep inside her.

You can do it, she told herself. *You must.*

Chapter 16 - 6:45 A.M.

Later, when she finally began thinking more rationally, she realized what needed to be done.

She had to get out of here. She hadn't heard them since the big one—Ice?—had reported his horrible message to the boy—Jett?—but she was reasonably certain they were still in the house.

Of course they're still here. This is all about money, isn't it? They're gonna stay here until the job is done...and if they think you're part of the job, then you really don't have much of a chance, do you?

She couldn't dwell on that. If she did, she'd be a basket case in minutes. No. She needed to focus. She began thinking of Craig again. Then, quite suddenly, a hot rage came from out of nowhere, singeing the back of her neck.

Damn him... If only he hadn't tricked me into coming out here in the first place...

Then, just as suddenly, the rage dissipated. Craig would want her to get out of this situation any way she could.

She forced herself to consider her predicament. If she could just lower the staircase contraption and ease on down...

There was one major problem with that. She'd have to push it closed once she'd lowered herself. But that would be no problem—they all had chains hanging down. All she had to do was grab hold of it and ease it back up.

105

The bad thing would be the time element involved. And it would also have to be done silently. Any noise she made would be heard, regardless of where the two men were or what they were doing.

Unless, of course, they were asleep.

If they were escapees from the West Virginia State Penitentiary, they'd both be light sleepers. Prisoners didn't have the luxury of sleeping soundly. They'd get their throats cut.

She decided against going down—at least, for the moment.

What was her other option? Stay here? Wait them out?

What if they decided to conduct another search?

Bobbie fought down another urge to scream. She reminded herself that screaming would serve no useful purpose and would only get her killed. She closed her eyes and forced herself to breathe more or less regularly.

Keep thinking. Don't ever stop. Once you stop, you might as well just go on down there right now and let them do what they want.

Using her penlight, she got up slowly and began looking around for something she could use as a weapon.

***

Jett stopped moving. His face tilted upwards.

"What's up?" Ice asked.

"Think I heard somethin'."

Ice looked up at the ceiling and remained still for nearly half a minute. "Don't hear nothin'." He moved quietly to the front window and carefully eased the tattered drape open an inch or so. It was still dark. The porch light splashed the front and part of the woody knoll on the other side of the drive. He shook his head and let go of the drape. Then turned and went over to the doorway.

"Maybe I just had a bad dream." Jett rubbed his eyes. He knew that wasn't far from the truth. He had some nasty dreams, mostly about Momma and her boyfriends.

Lately, his "falling" dream had been coming back.

He didn't mind most of the others, but when the "falling" dream came back, things got hairy. He didn't know why, but when he dreamed of falling, he always woke up in a cold sweat, sometimes with wet pants, looking around for Momma. Afterward, he had a pounding headache that lasted most of the day.

The dream he really liked was the new one he started having when he'd first started hanging around Ice. The two of them were riding choppers, with leather-clad ladies clinging to them as they came into town. The ladies were big-breasted and beautiful, screaming in ecstasy as Ice and Jett— genuine bad-assed dudes—rode their choppers just like in those old biker movies.

It was one cool dream. He wished he had it more often.

Ice came back into the hall, got his cigarettes from his pocket, shook one from the pack and lit it. "Go get some more shuteye. We'll start lookin' again in a bit." He glanced past Jett, toward the front door. "Don't think she drove up and changed her mind. I woulda heard."

Jett went back into the living room and lay down on the cushion. He closed his eyes and squirmed into a comfortable position. That pasta salad could be giving him indigestion. He'd heard that certain foods made you dream funny.

Pasta wasn't exactly Jett's favorite food.

Maybe this time he'd have a good dream—the one about the choppers and the ladies dressed in leather.

That would be okay—as long as he didn't fall in it.

Waking up with wet pants sure was embarrassing.

Chapter 17 - 7:15 A.M.

After another careful investigation, Bobbie reached the dismal conclusion that her choice of useful weapons was severely limited.

She'd examined two more boxes but found nothing other than old cookware and a few pots and pans. There were many other items packed beneath the cookware, but further examination would require enormous strength and care.

The frightening fact remained. Her only possible exit was down the staircase and, judging by what her instinct told her about the two men, this had to be done as soon as possible. As long as the two were in the house and moving around, her future was in severe jeopardy.

She got her bag ready, stuffing it tightly with her jacket so nothing would shift or spill outward if she fell or stumbled. Thanks to RAD Day, she was wearing her tennis shoes, rather than the two-inch spikes she usually wore to the office. While she'd always considered RAD Day silly and unprofessional, she knew that because of all this, she'd never again scoff at the idea of going to work dressed casually.

She shoved the screwdriver she'd found in her left rear pocket—handle first, so it wouldn't slide out. The curved handle of the crowbar protruded from her bag.

For the next ten minutes she eyed the peephole, watching for signs of life below. She heard only silence.

Were they still in the house?

Were they sleeping? If so, how much longer would she have before they woke up?

How long would it take her to inch open the staircase, climb down, ease it closed, sneak down the stairs, tiptoe to the screen door, open it, squeeze through, close it quietly behind her and dash down the hill?

What if she stumbled? Broke a toe? Twisted an ankle? What if—

Stop it.

Her heart thumping like a bass drum, Bobbie inched closer to the staircase trap. She got down on her knees and then shifted into the position that would enable her to push open the trapdoor of the attic staircase.

Moments later, holding her breath, she pushed the door open two—then three—inches.

Then she heard their voices directly below.

***

"Where you goin', kid?"

"I'm still hungry, Ice. That pasta didn't set too well." Jett headed for the kitchen.

Sighing, Ice got up, went over to the curtains, and had another look at the wooded front of the property. Seeing nothing out of the ordinary, he went outside and stood on the porch step, listening.

Nothing. He turned and went back inside. Before going down the hall, he stopped cold and looked up at the staircase. He stood stock-still,

110

listening, trying to pick up the slightest disturbance. Then he tilted his head back and began staring at that attic panel. Something about it nagged at him.

The kitchen toilet flushed. Jett came out of the bathroom. Ice heard him opening the microwave door. The aroma of shrimp drifted out into the hall.

Realizing just how hungry he was, he remembered the burgers they'd had hours ago and licked his lips.

Jett was leaning against the kitchen counter. Ice lit a cigarette and rubbed the back of his neck. It was already nearly half past seven and, due to the thick fog, still moderately dark.

"What's up?" Munching on a piece of shrimp, Jett held another piece carefully between the thumb and index finger of his right hand.

Puffing on his cigarette, Ice went over to the bay window and scowled at the fog-laden darkness. Then he approached the sink and squashed his smoke in the drain. "If only that bastard hadn't up and died on us."

Jett didn't reply.

"If she was comin' out here to meet him, she woulda been here long before now."

Jett nodded.

"Then where the hell is she?"

Jett stood there silently, staring at the shrimp in his hand.

"We checked the grounds, front and back. The house, upstairs and down. Where else could she be?"

Jett swallowed the shrimp with an audible gulp.

Ice pointed a thumb toward the kitchen doorway. "The attic. The only place we haven't checked. Damn thing's been buggin' me half to death. Any ladders in the cellar?"

Jett nodded.

"Go downstairs and look. If there's one down there, bring it up. Otherwise, we'll get one from the barn. If she's not in the attic, she's probably not in the house. We might have to go back outside in an hour or so with the truck and check out the road."

***

Holding her breath, Bobbie slowly and very carefully inched the trapdoor shut.

With a heart-wrenching sigh of relief, she rolled on her back. Breathing heavily, she lay very still on the plywood sheet next to the trap.

The throbbing in her leg from its tense position had finally ebbed. She pulled it gingerly toward her, reached up and massaged the razor-like tingling in her calf.

Luckily, the big ape called Ice hadn't looked up. Otherwise…

She forced her thoughts away from that. She had to keep all distractions and fears at bay while concentrating on getting out of here.

But how could she reach a safe place? She was hiding in an attic. The only opening consisted of an air vent about one foot square, screened and hidden behind two boxes stacked with tools, cookware, books, garbage, and God only knew what else. The cast-iron pots and pans weighed a ton and would make enough racket, if disturbed, to wake the dead. The trusses and rafters above her head went to the roof, which looked in fine shape. There were no cracks, holes, or deterioration. The Gelts had obviously paid to have the roof redone not long ago.

There was nowhere to go but down. Like it or not, her only means of escape was through the attic door.

Before the cold, harsh pang of desperation shot through her, she heard the echoing roar of the toilet flushing below her.

Her heart fluttering, she rolled over and positioned her right eye directly above her makeshift peephole. Ice was standing halfway up the staircase, staring up at her.

Her pulse raced and her body turned ice-cold. She thought of Craig and a warm pang of regret washed deeply inside her gut.

No one deserved to die like that. No one.

She rubbed her eyes and told herself not to dwell on that. If she managed to get out of here, she was going to look at a lot of things differently.

Moments later, after her nerves had settled and she felt more in control, she lowered her face to her peephole.

Ice had disappeared.

For a moment she felt honest relief. But reality quickly returned, and she knew she shouldn't lower her guard. In this situation, not seeing or hearing them didn't mean anything good. In fact, she had the eerie feeling that something bad was about to happen.

She tried to convince herself it was just her imagination working overtime again. However, something deep inside her told her she was being unduly optimistic.

She closed her eyes and told herself things would be okay. Just because the big brute was no longer standing on the step didn't exactly mean doom was on its way. They might have decided to venture outside again. They might have even decided to steal Craig's Porsche and leave for good.

No. That alone made no sense. They'd been paid by someone to come here and kill Craig. There was no way they'd just leave without making sure she was nowhere to be found.

A sudden heavy thumping below her interrupted her thoughts. Startled, she peered through the peephole again.

The one called Jett was rushing up the steps.

He was carrying a *ladder*!

Chapter 18 - 7:30 A.M.

As Jett sprinted past carrying a paint-spattered stepladder, Ice went back downstairs to check the front yard through the living room window.

It was getting light, but the fog still hadn't burned off the tops of the trees in the valley. The panoramic view was splashed with a grayish hue. However, that wasn't what had caught his attention the moment he parted the drapes. It was something down the hill from where the Porsche was parked. A sound coming from outside had made him flinch. It was the angry barking of a dog.

"Jett!"

The boy was standing on the top step, holding the ladder.

Ice gestured. "Put that ladder down and get down here. Quick."

Jett opened the ladder, set it on the floor behind him and hurried back downstairs. "What's up, Ice?"

"Somethin's out there." Ice went over to the screen door and listened.

"The lady?"

"Might be." Ice had already fetched the roll of duct tape from his jacket pocket. "Maybe a stray spotted her." The revolver materialized in his right hand. He turned to Jett. "You veer off to the left, I'll head to the right. We'll move right down that hill. We can fan out and cover twice as much ground. It's gettin' light, so we'll be able to see things pretty damn soon."

115

"Want me to yell if I see her, Ice?"

"Yeah. Then we'll bring her back here." He grinned. "We'll take her upstairs, dump her on the bed and have some fun." Ice turned serious. "Let's go."

Without another word they slipped out through the screen door.

***

A cold shiver washed through Bobbie when Jett opened the ladder directly below her. She knew then that her time was almost up, and those two would find her in just minutes.

So why did he suddenly rush back downstairs?

She wanted to push open the trap a couple of inches so she could hear what was going on.

That wouldn't be very bright. She wasn't sure how much they could see from the foot of the stairs. For all she knew, they could be looking directly at the attic.

She kept at her post for five minutes, her right eye directly over the peephole. She saw nothing, heard nothing. A few moments later she thought she heard what sounded like a screen door easing shut.

Her heart thundered. Had they left? Was it possible her luck had just changed?

She couldn't let herself think that. If she let down her guard, she'd be dead.

Something had obviously distracted them; she was sure of it.

Now she had to decide what could be going on and what she should do. She knew only that she didn't have much time to think of a solution.

***

Jett reached the bottom of the wooded hill and began looking around for signs of the lady.

Just a few yards away, the narrow creek disappeared into the sloping countryside. He could see portions of the main road about fifty yards away, behind the trees. As he moved carefully through the overgrown brush, he kept catching his pant legs on briars and sharp twigs from dead limbs.

So far, he'd seen nothing but brown grass, yellowish-brown leaves, and deadfalls. He couldn't imagine anyone hiding out here.

As Ice had said, this lady was a city gal. City gals hated getting dirty. A city gal wouldn't be running around out here in the woods anyway—especially if she was wearing spike heels.

Momma didn't even want to go out in the yard when she was all gussied up. She said her makeup would run if she stayed out too long in the sunlight. She couldn't even tuck Jett in before she left for the night when she'd just done her nails and couldn't touch anything till they dried. Momma and Fay and their other girlfriends all looked the same when they were out, their wigs brushed and fluffed and sprayed, their jewelry dancing brightly on their wrists, fingers, and necks. They also highlighted their cleavages with makeup and cleaned and ironed their dresses so they didn't show a smudge or wrinkle.

Jett moved along the underbrush and thought about his momma…how those grim-looking people in white uniforms came to the house and took her away when she was going through that bad spell. That was when they'd stuck Jett in one of those

117

crowded homes while Momma was getting well. He hadn't made any friends there. He figured it was because he was a couple years older than most of the other kids. Since he'd always been a loner, it hadn't bothered him much. He kept to himself and patiently waited for Momma to come back and take him home.

Now he was looking for someone just like Momma, only this lady was scared and hungry. She was probably hiding because she might have seen them taping up her boyfriend and knew they'd do the same thing with her.

Jett suddenly had a vision of Ice finding this lady, and when he brought her back to the house, she looked just like Momma.

He felt hot and tingly, like the time he'd scalded himself with the steam iron when he wasn't watching what he was doing.

He wouldn't like it if Ice got hold of Momma, ripped off her clothes and slipped it to her after he'd tied her up. It would be just like the time that bastard Reagan took Momma into the bedroom and started beating her around after he'd been out drinking all night.

Suddenly tense and nervous, Jett crept silently up the hill, searching for the lady.

Maybe if he found her first, he could make things right.

***

A mongrel dog jumped out of the bush just as Ice reached the bottom of the hill.

A quivering brown speckled rabbit with glossy, unseeing eyes twitched helplessly in the dog's

118

clenched jaws. Eyeing Ice guardedly, the ratty mastiff-pit mix growled softly before backing up slowly, then turning around and darting into the woods.

Ice lowered the revolver and frowned.

A stupid mongrel *dog*, dammit.

All that commotion over a damn *mutt* huntin' down a stupid rabbit.

"Jett!" He turned around and faced the hill. "Go on back to the house! It was just a goddamn dog!"

Chapter 19 - 8:00 A.M.

After furious deliberation, Bobbie decided to return to the other attic trap.

It would be too difficult and time-consuming to descend the attic with the stepladder the boy had placed directly underneath. If she stumbled or lost her balance, she wouldn't have a prayer.

It only took her a minute or two to crawl back. Once she'd positioned herself next to the wooden panel, she spent several precious minutes deciding what to do with her bag. Should she discard it? It was much too big and heavy to lug around. If she left it in the attic, they'd eventually find it. Then they'd know for certain that she'd been up here.

If she wanted to get away fast, she had to travel light.

She decided to dump it someplace they'd already checked. Underneath the bed seemed logical. If she could make it to the first floor, she could hide it under the living room couch.

But no matter what she decided, she had to move quickly. After the two had gone outside, she'd heard nothing. She had no idea how long they'd be gone but knew they'd be back. She had to get out of the attic before they returned.

She wouldn't need much time. Once she climbed down, she could leave the house and make it to the woods in just a couple of minutes. Since this place was a good twenty minutes by car from civilization, she was facing quite a run. All she needed was a few minutes' head start. She could be out of sight long before they returned.

Using the screwdriver, she pried open the trap and forced her shoulder bag through. Then, after listening to the silence for another minute, she managed to squeeze her slim figure through the opening.

Once she was sitting on the top shelf, she twisted around and tried getting the trap closed again. To her horror, she found that she could only lower it until it was about six inches from being closed.

Panic riveted through her. She had visions of them finding her lying there, her fingers caught in the opening.

Her mind racing, she pushed the trap open and pulled it back down. It was still a tight fit, but she managed to close it until her fingertips were squeezed snugly in the tiny gap.

Once again, she pushed the trap open. When she pulled it back down again, it closed all the way.

She sighed in relief. When she looked down, she saw that the bottom shelf was dangling, nearly torn free of its hinges. Ice had obviously put his weight on it.

She flipped around. Then, facing the top shelf, she slid down until her feet were just above the floor. Very carefully she lowered herself until her tennis shoes reached the floor.

For seconds she didn't move. She just stood there, listening to the silence.

She heard only the distant barking of a dog.

Taking a deep breath, Bobbie snatched up her bag, slipped out of the closet and came face to face with Craig's lifeless body lying on the bed. The tape over his mouth had been peeled halfway back. His mouth, chin, and both cheeks were covered with a snotty-colored sheen. More of the stuff was smeared on the pillow beside his face.

Her heart sputtered. She covered her mouth and forced the scream back down. This wasn't the time for a good scream. Craig was dead. His worries were over. Hers, on the other hand, were very real.

She turned away quickly and tried to ignore what she'd just seen, but their final argument came back, and she remembered how the man had been, standing there in the hall, hurt and betrayed...

She forced it out of her head. Then she crossed the room and stopped cold.

Heavy footsteps thundered from the front porch.

***

Ice stopped in the entranceway and fitted a cigarette carefully into a corner of his mouth.

As he lit it, he stared up the staircase. "Right now, we're gonna see what's in that damn attic," he said softly, a dark look taking over his rugged features.

Jett began thinking of his momma again. He couldn't imagine what he could do to prevent Ice from raping and killing her. He only knew how badly he'd feel if he stood right there like a moron and let his big friend kill Momma. He could never look at Ice again after that.

Not *your momma*, a voice inside him said.

Not even a friend of Momma's.

His mind had been playing tricks on him again. It was doing one of those topsy-turvy things, as it always did when he was confused. When that happened, he couldn't tell what was real and what was going on in his mind. Right now, he saw himself and Ice finding this city gal, tying her to the bed, ripping her clothes off and having the time of their lives. Jett and Ice doing what they pleased because they were a team…and because they split things right down the middle. Five-oh, five-oh.

Jett smiled impishly. The confusion was gone, and the only thing he noticed now was a strange hot feeling in his crotch when he whispered, "Let's find her, Ice."

***

Bobbie frantically investigated the bedroom window. She kept telling herself not to turn around. If she didn't turn around, she'd be okay.

The window was solid, made many years ago, possibly when the house was built. She tried turning the catch. It wouldn't budge and seemed welded in position. She tried again, using her thumb and the meaty side of her index finger, applying pressure until the sharp cramping in her knuckles made her stop.

She tried using the screwdriver in her pocket, but her efforts were fruitless. She studied it closely, noting the coats of paint slapped over the works. Green, yellow, blue, and gold peeked out in wavy layers. She gritted her teeth and tried once more.

Just then, she froze in her efforts.

They were coming up the stairs.

123

As Ice scaled the steps, he found that he was getting really tired.

This cat-and-mouse game was costing them time and a shitload of money. The Man obviously had no idea what was going on. If that chick had come out here, they would've found her by now. There was no way she could hide from them this long.

But even so, they had to make damn sure. What if she *had* come out here with Sheffield, seen them from a window and found a place to hide? What if she'd somehow escaped during the night? She might have crawled somewhere safe, then lay low and split at the first opportunity. She was a material witness, and could put them both in the chair...

He'd told himself a long time ago that they'd never take him again. He'd swallow a bullet first. Luckily, they'd got him for the smaller stuff—racketeering and extortion—and hadn't been able to nail him for capital murder. If they ever found what was left of Gina, those offed bikers or the gang punks he'd chopped up and put in dumpsters all over Allegheny County, he'd be totally fucked.

A new breed was walking around these days. He'd seen some of them in the pen and figured they couldn't have been much more than twenty years old. Gang members. Psycho killers. The same breed of animal the Tong used in big cities nowadays. The Tong used illegals, barely old enough to have a hard-on. But they'd decapitate a three-month-old baby if they were told to, and without batting an eye.

Ice pulled the revolver out of his waistband and broke it open. Six slugs. One for him, one for the kid. If they got caught, he'd feed the kid a quick one and dust a cop or two before giving himself one in the head.

Ice reached the landing. When he thought of climbing up to the attic to look for Sheffield's chick, he felt the anger coming back.

***

Trembling, Bobbie lay on her stomach under the bed, more frightened than she'd ever been in her entire life.

Right now, she couldn't hear anything but the heavy pounding of her heart in her ears. She knew they were upstairs; she'd just heard them coming up. They were probably on the landing, doing something with the ladder. They might be getting ready to lower the attic staircase.

The staircase came with a long pull chain— why would they need a ladder?

Her thoughts stopped abruptly when they came into the room. The kid approached the bed and stood just five feet away, his beat-up tennis shoes frightening close.

Bobbie prayed that they didn't drop anything— that nothing would put them at her level.

The tennis shoes moved away with a barely audible *squish*.

"What's wrong, kid?" Ice had walked over to the closet door. "Stiff ain't gonna bother nobody."

"Gives me the creeps, the way he's layin' there, lookin' at the ceiling."

Ice barked laughter. "Get a grip, kid. Let's see if I can crawl up that damn attic panel this time." The big leather work boots moved toward the closet doorway.

Bobbie stifled a gasp. She was sure that if they investigated the panel closely, they'd realize it had been moved. Her thoughts raced, and her heart continued pounding furiously. She wanted to see what they were doing but knew she shouldn't move. She didn't want to give them any excuse to glance below the bedspread.

"Gonna use the ladder, Ice?" the boy asked.

"Don't need it. Closet's got shelves I can stand on."

Ten seconds of silence. Then, a loud creaking sound.

Seconds later, a sharp crack, followed a violent crash, shook the floor.

Bobbie figured the big ape had probably broken the bottom shelf with his mammoth weight.

"God*dammit*!"

"What happened, Ice?"

"Damn shelf gave way. I can't push the damn trap open if the shelves won't hold my weight."

"Too heavy, Ice?"

"Ya think?"

The kid's tennis shoes began backing up toward the doorway.

Ice said, "Maybe I oughta bring in that ladder after all, then—"

He suddenly went silent.

Bobbie held her breath.

126

"Ladder's too tall, Ice. I don't think we'll be able to get it in there and open it—"

"Yeah, that would probably piss me off even worse. I guess I need to check out the other trap first. Don't know how anybody could get up there when the chain's missin', but that damn thing's been buggin' me."

Bobbie choked down a groan. There was no chain. *My God*... And she nearly tried going down that way...

"Maybe the chain was there when she first went up," the kid said.

"Howzat?"

"Maybe she pulled it down, climbed up, and yanked off the chain when she pulled it closed."

A short pause. "How'd she pull it closed?"

"I...dunno, Ice..."

Another short pause. "She mighta ripped off the chain first, climbed up and then pulled it shut."

"I guess she coulda done that..."

"Let's check it out."

Bobbie couldn't pull her gaze from the two pairs of shoes shuffling out of the room.

***

Ice adjusted the ladder and made sure the metal braces were extended straight out and locked, ready to take his weight.

He pulled the gun from his waistband and turned to Jett. "Go get my flashlight," he whispered. "I think I left it on the kitchen counter."

"Wh-Why the gun, Ice?" Jett asked uneasily.

Ice shook his head. Sometimes the kid showed a couple of actual working brain cells. Other times, he stayed a total moron. "Want me to get my throat cut when I crawl up there? There could be all kinds of shit stored up there in the attic. What if she found a weapon?"

"Never thought of *that*, Ice…"

"Well, now you have somethin' to think about."

When the boy turned, Ice caught him by the crook of the arm. "While you're downstairs, get the clothesline I got in the back of the pickup. We'll need to slip somethin' through that eyehook to get the door open."

***

One of them rushed down the stairs.

Bobbie could tell by the light sound that it was the boy. She assumed Ice was still out in the hall.

All she could do was stay as quiet as possible. Lucky for her the bedspread hung low; otherwise, they'd be able to see her if they peered into the room.

On a whim, she slid over to the far side of the bed. Then, taking a portion of checkered spread and nudging it up an inch or so, she stuck her head out and peered upward.

Craig's lying dead on that mattress...

A warm sourness filled her throat. She swallowed and fought down a wave of warm dizziness. She told herself Craig was no longer feeling any pain…that he'd gone to a better world…that—

It was no use. She just couldn't get past the horrid fact that there was a corpse lying on the mattress above her…or that the corpse had once been her boss. He was the same man who'd hired

128

her...who'd been trying to hit on her the last six months.

Just hours ago, he was alive...

Don't go back there. Think of now...and the dangerous dilemma you're facing because of the man lying dead on the bed just above you. Because of his lies, his selfishness, and his obsession to get you between the sheets, he brought you to this isolated farmhouse --

Stop this and focus!

She eased the bedspread back down and forced her mind to start working again.

Chapter 20 - 8:30 A.M.

Jett held the clothesline as Ice positioned the ladder directly beneath the attic staircase. He watched closely as the big man jerked the ladder to make sure the metal brackets were locked.

As he worked, Ice kept staring at the attic panel. "It would be our luck if she changed her mind and decided not to come out here in the first place. But we gotta find out, once and for all."

Jett handed him the clothesline. Ice reached in his back pocket, pulled out his hunting knife, snapped it open and sliced off a four-foot length. He climbed the ladder, pushed the end through the eyehook and knotted it on the other side. He let the line hang free as he climbed back down and dragged the ladder out of the way. "*Now* we'll see what's up there."

Ice fitted the flashlight in his right armpit. Holding the gun steady in his right hand, the big man used his left hand to reach for the line. "Stand back," he whispered. "If she's up there, she might be waitin' to toss somethin' down."

Jett moved awkwardly to the side.

Ice grasped the line. In one sweeping motion, he yanked the trap open. It whooshed down, stopping abruptly, and bobbing about four feet above the floor.

Ice quickly moved behind it and pointed the gun straight up. For tense moments he stood completely still, waiting for something to move near the opening.

The rectangular hole stared blankly down at them.

A full minute later, Ice circled around to the foot of the wooden stairs. He continued looking up, keeping the gun pointed at the opening. He grasped the flashlight and aimed it straight up. Then, after about another minute, he stuck it back in his armpit. Using his left hand, he pulled out the lower section of stairs and backed up. It snapped open, the bottom step bobbing just a foot or so above the floor.

Ice pointed the flashlight directly at the opening.

"Ice?"

"Quiet."

"I just think—"

Ice spun around and pointed the light in Jett's face. The harsh yellow light forced his eyes shut. Things began moving around inside his head like sparklers. Ice's mouth was just a couple of inches away. Jett couldn't see it because of all the lights, but he could smell that stale-cigarette-and-whiskey odor he always smelled on Ice.

"I'm goin' up there." Ice's voice had turned into a soft, low growl. "You got somethin' to say? Wait till I check the attic—understand?"

"S-Sure, Ice."

The flashlight was lowered.

Jett blinked and saw bunches of little brownish-red dots bobbing all over the place. Ice tapped him on the back of the head. Jett squinted at him. Ice's face was fixed in one of those strained grins beyond the fading dots.

"Why do ya have to piss me off, kid?" Ice playfully mussed Jett's hair.

Jett shrugged. He didn't want to say the wrong thing—especially since the sparklers had set off a nagging ache in the back of his head.

"What'll I do when you're up there, Ice?" he asked.

"Stay here and…" Ice stopped talking and turned toward the bedroom. He grinned again, like he always did when he had a brainstorm. "Go on in there and keep the old boy company."

Jett swallowed. "S-Seriously, Ice?"

"He ain't gonna bite."

Jett felt something sour moving around in the pit of his stomach. Being in that room with a dead guy… It sounded freaky.

"Listen, kid." Ice lowered his voice. "That stiff's worth a hundred grand. Think of it. A hundred thousand smackeroos. That's fifty thousand apiece." His grin stretched wide across his face. "Ya know what you can buy with fifty grand?"

Jett began thinking about that chopper he'd been dreaming about, but his thoughts immediately shifted to those hookers they'd seen at Fancy Dan's. Especially the redhead. A hooker might not be as great as a chopper, but with fifty grand, he and Ice could get both.

Still, the idea of sitting in a room with a stiff made him feel like something was crawling all over him. "Ice, I dunno if I can—"

Ice's hand closed on Jett's shoulder, sending a sharp cluster of hot pain down Jett's arm. "Kid, it's time to get serious. Go on in there right now, sit down and stay outa my way. I'll call ya if I need ya."

Jett thought over Ice's reasoning. He knew he'd been messing up, and he surely didn't want to get in Ice's way—especially with that much money at stake.

As the big man carefully ascended the attic stairs, Jett turned arduously to the bedroom doorway, where the stiff lay on the big double bed.

***

The boy Jett came into the bedroom doorway and stopped about ten feet away, staring at the bed.

Shivering, Bobbie kept her gaze fixed on the tennis shoes…the long-looped laces dangling over the sides…the faded jeans.

Please oh please *turn around and go away…*

The tennis shoes shuffled closer to the bed.

My dear God…

Bobbie stayed near the far side of the bed and clenched her jaw tight to keep her teeth from chattering.

The boy took a few more steps. Soon he'd be very close to the edge of the bed. Bobbie could clearly see the scuff marks on the round white toes of the tennis shoes. The laces practically brushed the floor and were flecked with dirt.

Outside in the grass, she realized grimly. He'd dirtied his shoes while he and that big brute were taping up Craig.

Just then, he began mumbling. "Ice w-wants me to st-stay in here with you." He was obviously very nervous. "Sorry, but I just can't do this. I can't…I just can't…" The tennis shoes turned away from the bed. The boy pulled the chair toward the doorway. The harsh sound of the chair dragging across the wooden floor stung her ears like an army of hornets. He turned the chair around and sat ass-backwards, facing the hall.

Bobbie didn't think he'd turn around. He was quite possibly doing what he needed to do to cope with the situation. It wasn't much different from what she'd herself done just a few minutes earlier. She sensed that he wasn't a killer at all—that he was just along for the ride.

That didn't make sense, did it? If these two had come here because they were being paid to kill Craig and her as well, they were both killers. And even if the boy got a little queasy being in the same room with a corpse, that didn't necessarily mean he wasn't a killer. Killers weren't exactly the most stable people on earth. If they were, they wouldn't be killing others for money.

Bobbie suddenly realized that she was grasping the crowbar protruding from her bag. It frightened her that she'd unconsciously reached for it. It must have been a self-survival reaction she'd never had cause to use before. Whatever it was, she chose to go with it. Luckily, her denim jacket slid out easily, without a sound. She laid it on the floor beside her. The crowbar came out like a warm knife gliding through soft margarine.

Thank God the big ape was in the attic, making the ceiling creak. His movements would muffle any sound she might make.

Gripping the crowbar, she began crawling out from underneath the bed. Unless the boy turned around, he'd be facing the other direction.

Bobbie emerged from under the bed. She stayed near the wooden frame, curled in a tight crouch, her nerves hammering like knife blades raking her skin. She stayed right there, watching him, too paralyzed to move.

Did she really have to do this?

Yes. It was necessary. If she wimped out, he'd yell for his friend and that would be the ball game.

Trembling, she straightened.

The boy sat quite still. If she knocked him out, she wondered if he'd cause a loud thud when he fell out of the chair…if his friend would hear it from the attic.

Maybe she should wait.

For what? And why? Was it because physical violence nauseated her? Just a couple of hours ago, she'd slapped Craig, hadn't she?

She'd only done that in self-defense. It was sheer instinct. She'd lashed out to keep him away from her…to keep him from…

From what? Slapping her around? Manhandling her? Craig just wasn't the physical type. He was a dog, and cheated on his wife…but aside from that, he was a gentleman, and he would have never resorted to physical violence to—

Stop this. It isn't the right time for it.

135

She took three slow, cautious steps. When she was less than three feet from the boy, the floorboard beneath her left foot creaked just loud enough to cause the boy to stiffen.

A moment later, he jerked his head in her direction.

Chapter 21 - 8:45 A.M.

Jett heard something behind him and cringed.

He swallowed hard, gripping the wooden arms of the chair. This didn't make sense. Corpses couldn't move or make noises. Corpses were dead. They couldn't do anything but just lie there...

Could they?

But that noise... He was positive he'd heard something behind him.

Maybe he was hearing things again. Or maybe the house was just making old-house noises.

He began thinking of that giant rat again. He tried to remember if that house had creaked any, but his mind had suddenly gone blank.

A moment later, despite his inhibitions, he jerked his head a few inches to the right. Out of the corner of his eye, he could see the table next to the bed, the head of the bed and the blurry shape lying on it.

The man was dead. There was no way he'd get up and start walking again...or make creaking noises.

Maybe it was that weird thing in his head doing this. It could be all those years of being told how stupid he was...being told by Momma, her boyfriends. Here he was with Ice, learning all about things, and a stiff was making him as jumpy as a jackrabbit.

Jett had never actually been near a corpse before. He'd seen people being beaten up all the time. Hell, he'd seen Momma beaten up a dozen times.

Why, then, was he suffering from a case of the jitters?

He'd just have to get over this. When you whack folks for a living, you can't let stuff bother you. When they're dead, they're dead, and they sure can't do anything—even when they're lying on the bed just a few feet away.

He sighed, looked down at his lap and caught a glimpse of the shoelace on his left tennis shoe. Damn thing had loosened and was dragging the floor. He needed to tie it. Otherwise, he'd end up tripping over it as he'd done a zillion times before. Besides, it would give him something to do. And when he was through, he'd stand up like a man, walk over to that corpse, look it right in the eye and tell it there was no way it would spook him ever again.

Jett took a deep breath. Then he bent and reached down to fix his shoelace.

A second later, he heard another creak—this one closer and louder than the first one.

His face grew very warm. Then, just as he turned once again to see what had made the noise, the back of his head exploded in a blinding-white jolt of pain.

Everything turned black, melting into a warm haze.

***

When the boy had turned his head, Bobbie had been out of his peripheral range. All he'd seen, she guessed, was the bed, Craig, and the wall behind the bed.

She didn't budge—or even breathe—until the boy turned back around. Then he bent forward in the chair. It looked like he was reaching for something. She saw him doing something with his tennis shoe. This put him in the same position as before, but much lower. It would give him less distance to fall, making it easier for her to do this quietly.

She raised her trembling arm. The crowbar was now ready for serious business. She hesitated one last time, wondering if she should do it. She knew she had no choice, and if she didn't do it, it could mean her death.

She took three quick, heart-stopping steps toward the boy. Once again, her shoe made a creaking sound on the floor.

Her blood jolted at the sound—a heavy throb that instantly turned to ice. But she ignored it as she raised the crowbar another couple of inches. Then, before she could make another move, the boy turned in her direction once again, and this time she realized she had to follow through with this. Holding her breath, she brought the round end of the crowbar down in an arc that trembled slightly. She felt herself pulling away, directing it several inches from the intended target. Even so, it sliced through the air, cracking the back of the boy's skull an instant before it could steer clear of its intended path.

The boy gasped weakly. He shuddered, collapsing, and sliding—freely, as if he were made of liquid foam—quietly to the floor. His head bobbed loosely. His left arm dropped, knuckles lightly rapping the floorboards.

He lay on his back, not moving.

For several seconds, Bobbie also did not move. Then she began shivering as if she'd just been splashed with ice water.

Then, just as she lowered her trembling arm to her side, Ice began yelling from the attic.

**

"Kid! I think someone's been up here!"

Ice could feel it in his bones. It was nothing obvious—just that inner sense that nipped at him when something wasn't quite right.

It might've been that vague lavender scent he'd caught when he'd first come up. And, judging by those neat piles stacked near the boxes, it sure looked like someone had been sniffing around.

Something wedged behind one of the boxes caught his eye.

An old Mason jar.

He bent over and aimed the light. Then he laid the revolver on the plywood, reached out and yanked the jar free. He examined it closer and turned it in his palm. Intrigued, he brought the flashlight closer. About two inches of some golden liquid sloshed around inside the jar. A wadded-up Kleenex floated around in its center.

Forgetting where he was, Ice stood and banged his head on an overhead cross beam. Cursing, he lowered his head, reached down, picked up the gun, and stuck it in his waistband. He unscrewed the lid.

140

He didn't have to stick his face closer to tell what was inside.

"Piss." He screwed the lid back on. "That chick took a leak in this jar." The liquid was strong and fairly fresh. She'd been up here, all right. The neat piles told him she'd been rummaging through the boxes, looking for something to piss in.

The image of it made his juices heat up again.

"Jett!" His booming voice echoed in the confined space. "We were right. She was up here all along!" He dropped the jar onto the plywood. It landed on its side and rolled back and forth, the liquid splashing against its sides.

For all they knew, she could still be in the house.

Without hesitation, he rushed over to the trapdoor and began climbing down the attic staircase.

***

The moment Bobbie heard him shouting from the attic, she stepped over the fallen boy and hurried over to the stairs. Then, as quietly as possible, she dashed down the steps.

The front entrance was just ten feet or so from the foot of the stairs. She ran over, cracked open the screen door, squeezed through and eased it closed.

A wash of warm relief flooded through her the instant her tennis shoe touched the cracked, aged wood of the front porch. She skipped down the steps and hurried over to the Porsche. Her heart was hammering as she bent to see if the keys were dangling from the ignition. It took her only a moment to discover that they were gone.

141

Undaunted, she circled the small car and made her way down the steep hill that led down the wooded slope.

As she hopped down the steep, grassy incline, she thought of nothing but getting away. Everything else had ceased to exist.

She'd even forgotten all about the crowbar still gripped tightly in her right hand.

***

His gut heating up, Ice carefully rolled Jett over.

A blackish-red crack bulged brightly at the crown of the boy's skull. The damn thing was nearly two inches long and looked like a lightning bolt. There wasn't much blood, but the knot underneath it was the size of a golf ball sliced in half. The boy was still breathing, but he'd been belted good. It would be a while before he came to.

As Ice straightened, he had a sudden flash of what was left of his brother Lonnie lying on the cold, glassy pavement after the semi had run him over. His scalp buzzed; he fought down the anger as he gazed down at the unconscious figure.

Seconds later, Lonnie turned back into Jett, and Ice knew he had to start focusing again. Jett was a good kid; he did whatever you told him to do. Even if he did come to, he'd be as useful as a rubber crutch.

Ice had to face facts. He was going to have to finish this job by himself, and he might even have to finish off the kid once he'd caught up to the bitch and brought her back.

He took one last look at Jett. A batch of fresh anger bubbled up, and his hands turned into tight fists as he hurried down the stairs.

Chapter 22 - 9:00 A.M.

Managing long, graceful strides, Bobbie kept up a steady clip through the hilly terrain.

She was relieved that her high school training had kicked in. In those days, she'd been one of Fox Chapel High's finest in track & field, competing in state competition. It was surprisingly easy for her to make believe the deadfalls blocking her path were hurdles in an obstacle course. Although she hadn't done any serious long-distance running for several years, this brought back the same feeling of invigoration, bombarding her bloodstream with fresh endorphins.

But that fantasy moment soon passed. When it did, the reason for her running flooded back into her head with such a jolt, it upset her timing—and her balance. She stubbed her toe on a jutting root hidden amongst the tall weeds and plummeted to the ground in a tangle of flying limbs.

She lay still for long, agonizing moments, trying to catch her breath. When she finally sat up, she brought up her wrist and stared in disbelief at the gouge the sharp tip of the screwdriver had made.

Enraged, she yanked it out of her back pocket and tossed it in the weeds. Then she examined her wrist and saw that the gouge was mostly superficial. The smallest drop of blood clung to a tiny torn flap of skin near the opening. She brought up her hand and gingerly sucked the gash, then cradled her throbbing toe while cursing herself for her clumsiness.

With some difficulty, she twisted around in the direction of the house. Luckily, the woods were thick enough to keep her hidden while she made for the highway—wherever *that* was...

But by the same token, the woods also hid *him*. For all she knew, he could be less than a hundred yards away, gaining headway rapidly.

Sensing the wave of panic approaching, she stood up carefully. There was an initial twang at first, but not bad enough to restrict her movements. She told herself it might ease up if she kept her weight off it.

But how do you keep your weight off one foot when you're running?

One thing worked in her favor: at least her appetite had scuttled off quietly into the shadows. The last thing in the world she needed right now was food...

But she sure was thirsty.

Oh, for a sip of fresh water...

The crowbar lay just ten feet away, half-hidden in bushes. She grabbed it and began moving away, this time with a pronounced limp. When the throbbing finally began to subside, she put more weight on it. After about fifty yards or so, the pain was still noticeable, but tolerable.

Bobbie increased her pace. A few minutes later, she was tearing through the woods.

***

As Ice reached the bottom of the staircase, he wondered once again if the woman was still hiding in the house.

It stood to reason that she'd want him to *think* she'd left. If so, her best bet was to lay low.

However, logic steered him in the opposite direction. Why would she stick around if she had even the slightest chance of getting away?

He felt his blood boiling when he thought of the kid lying unconscious at the top of the stairs. He forced himself to chill out and then stood perfectly still, listening. Hearing nothing, he took a few cautious steps and peered into the living room doorway.

The empty room sneered at him.

He decided she was just too smart and too frightened to try something that dangerous. She'd want as far away as possible. He opened the screen door, went out and stood on the front porch, carefully scanning the woods. He knew she wouldn't do well. A city chick surviving out here? Especially a *scared* city chick?

The idea was laughable.

That bitch has good reason to be scared. You don't scramble my little buddy's brains and expect to come out of it alive...

Chapter 23 - 9:30 A.M.

A shallow stream glittering in the morning light cut through the clearing at the bottom of the hill.

Bobbie sighed in relief at the wonderful sight. She immediately slowed her pace and cautiously descended the weed-choked slope, glancing in every direction and listening. Confident that she was alone, she dropped the crowbar on the grass beside her. After another quick assessment of her surroundings, she knelt and lowered her face into the cool, clear water. Enjoying the vibrant tingling sensation on her skin, she splashed her neck and hair with the delightful elixir. Then, ignoring her aching feet, she stood up sharply.

She'd caught some briars along the way. They were razor-sharp, but this wasn't the time to worry about a little pain. She had to get as far away as possible. The mere thought that a paid killer was after her made her shudder. She picked up the crowbar and immediately thought of the boy. Her fine features formed a tight mask the instant it came back. Feeling nauseous, she dropped her arm and looked away. She couldn't look at it and wondered how she could even touch the thing. After all, she'd nearly killed someone with it.

But she hadn't *killed* the boy, had she? No. She refused to believe she had. She clearly recalled that very last second—pulling back ever-so-slightly…just enough so the boy's skull didn't take the full impact of the blow. Even in those horrible circumstances, she just couldn't do it. She was no killer.

But reality intervened, and with it came the horrifying sound of the crowbar cracking the boy's skull. The nausea overtook her, and she let go of it. Then she dropped to her knees and threw up.

It took her only a few moments to collect herself. She wiped her mouth with the back of her hand, spat out the sour taste, crawled over to the water and dipped her face once again in its coolness.

The frightening image of the big brute crept boldly into her thoughts, forcing her to her feet. She grabbed the crowbar and scurried into the brush.

***

Ice peered cautiously around the corner of the front porch and eyed the barn, wondering if she'd gone there to hide.

It didn't seem likely. The building was too close, for one thing. She'd probably already checked the Porsche for keys and decided there wasn't much else she could do but head out on foot.

He wondered if the barn had a hayloft she could hide in...

Maybe he'd have a look. He could grab a pitchfork and have some fun, poking around.

Chuckling at the thought, he went down the front steps. He was about to turn the corner when something caught his eye.

A fresh footprint pressed smack-dab in the center of the dirt drive displayed the unmistakable treads of a tennis shoe.

The kid's? He bent and studied it closer. Nope. Too damn small. There were other prints in the area—the kid's, no doubt—but his were much bigger. This was a tennis-shoe print, all right...but definitely a woman's. The toe pointed to the hill leading to the main road. Farther down, another print showed clearly in the dirt. He estimated the stride and figured six, maybe seven feet apart.

She was obviously running.

There were briars, thorns, rock, gravel, low-hanging limbs, exposed roots, and poison ivy in those woods. There were also ditches and holes in the ground, as well as unexpected slopes and ridges. A scared city broad running for her life wouldn't get very far before busting her ass—especially if she wasn't familiar with the area.

Ice crossed the walk and headed for the heavily wooded valley. The slope was steep but presented no problem. He'd already gone down there and knew what to expect. He moved slowly, leisurely. He could take his time. He wouldn't be surprised to see her lying at the bottom of the hill, out cold in the weeds.

City broads never knew how to function when they were out of their element. Gina had to be toted everywhere—even to the damn 7-Eleven at the end of the block. She was so fucking lazy that he'd often wondered how she found the energy to do her nails.

Gina was a city broad, too.

He couldn't help wondering how this bitch had the smarts to bring tennis shoes out here.

It didn't matter. He'd find her—no matter *what* she had on her feet.

Judging by the direction she was headed, he knew that she'd quickly discover very little traffic out here. Her best bet was to try that dairy farm Ice had spotted earlier. The place was at least six, maybe eight miles straight down the hill.

Either way, he'd find her.

Chapter 24 - 10:00 A.M.

Running in long, easy strides, Bobbie switched her mind off her nightmare and went back to senior high, the summer she'd been voted Homecoming Queen.

There she was, running like a gazelle over the professionally turned dirt track, her long, slender limbs flowing like those of a ballet dancer. Later that weekend, after winning all the awards that could have been won for her team, she sat on the red velvet throne at the Homecoming Ball, her pink and white chiffon gown whispering quietly over her tender skin. She'd saved up all year for that gown. She hadn't known at the time that just three hours after she'd entered the Holiday Inn that night for the ball, that same material would be lying in a discarded heap on the floor of her date's beloved classic '61 T-Bird.

She was reliving that disheartening night when she stumbled on a tangle of brush. After tripping and falling on her face, she rolled down the long grassy slope. Once the slope ended and the ground leveled, she stopped rolling and lay there, twenty yards from the clearing.

Bobbie lay on her back and did not move.

***

Ice trudged through the thick underbrush.

Every once in a while he spotted some small sign of recent activity—a broken twig, or mashed grass.

Since she was hauling ass, she wasn't leaving too much of a trail. Her strides seemed just as they'd been from the start. She was either a damned good runner or was scared shitless.

Ice liked them to be scared. When a chick was scared, it was more fun playing the game. It was the fear that made the body come alive. Everything turned bright and vivid and real. It was like looking at things through a powerful microscope.

Serial killers had the fear-thing down. They knew you were never more alive than when you were scared...when your pulse was thumping up a storm...when your knees were pounding a bongo beat...when you were just a hair short of pissing your drawers.

Gina had gone totally crazy when Ice had her staked out and began breaking her fingers, one by one. She'd let out one bloodcurdling scream after another even though he'd crammed three feet of bed sheeting down her throat and sealed her lips with two feet of duct tape. Her eyes were filled with terror, her skin covered with sweat, giving off a healthy pink glow. He'd never forget the plethora of smells emanating from her.

It was the smell of her fear, the sounds of her terror and the sight of her struggles that caused the adrenaline to explode inside him. Even though it was their last time, it was the best sex he'd ever had with her in the five years they were together.

Grinning at the memories, he climbed the next hill, stopped at the crest, and surveyed the valley. Aside from a few restless birds and occasional traffic sounds a few miles beyond the valley, he caught no sign of her. But he knew she wasn't far.

Chapter 25 - 11:15 A.M.

When Bobbie opened her eyes, the sun had filled the sky.

She tried raising an arm, but it weighed a ton. She tried raising it again. This time, it hovered just a few inches above the grass, trembling.

She tried studying her watch. She had to bring it closer than usual—the glare didn't help, and her vision was blurred. She couldn't read it, so she let her arm drop.

How long had she been out? An hour? Two hours?

My God...he could be on the other side of the hill!

Taking a deep breath, she lay very still, willing herself to recover. She remained like that for about a minute before she tried sitting up. It was an effort. Every muscle in her body ached. Her joints throbbed, and she feared that she'd twisted her spine in the fall. The toe she'd stubbed earlier had begun to swell.

She turned on her side and propped herself up. Woozy at first, she took another deep breath and began rubbing her ankles and toes. Her ankles had swelled, but she told herself she'd be okay. If only she could protect them somehow...

She eased painfully into a standing position and stood swaying as more dizziness rocked through her. She closed her eyes and waited for it to pass. Then she began checking for injuries. There was no blood, no torn clothing. She didn't think she'd suffered anything serious. She was grateful she could stand without help.

She tried a couple of steps. Aside from the swollen toe and protests from her cracking knees, she could still move around freely. Taking short, careful steps, she approached the pile of strewn trash that covered at least three hundred square feet of the clearing.

It didn't take her long to find a pile of rags made from bed sheeting. They lay in a collapsed box beneath a beat-up kitchen table and could be used to wrap her ankles.

She pulled some from the box and, using her penknife, tore a sheet into four two-inch-wide strips. She sat down in the soft grass and took off her tennis shoes. It only took a minute or so to wrap her feet, interlacing the strips around her toes and extending them around each pad, then above each ankle. She tied the loose ends snugly above the ankles, testing them to make sure they provided enough padding. Confident they'd suffice, she put her shoes back on and laced them somewhat loosely, to compensate for the sheeting.

Without dallying a moment longer, she straightened and began walking, lifting her feet just high enough to clear the exposed roots. It was a strange experience, but after fifty or sixty feet, she found that she was moving as good as ever. Her back twinged at each step, but she told herself it would be okay once she got out of here and had time to rest.

Mindful of each step, she moved swiftly back into the woods. She'd forgotten all about the crowbar, which she'd dropped in the tall grass when she'd fallen down the hill.

***

Jett opened his eyes and immediately felt an onslaught of agonizing pain.

His head throbbed mercilessly. A giant bright-red stabbing pain in his skull made him cringe.

He tried sitting up, but the pain made him cry out. Gingerly he reached up to feel the right side of his head, which throbbed with bright, excruciating pain. The moment his fingers touched a huge warm mass, he cried out. Sparklers had been sizzling inside him. He closed his eyes. When they finally settled down, he tried to remember where he was. Darkness filled his mind, and he began thinking of Momma and that guy who'd been spending time with her all summer. Jett didn't like him very much. This guy was always drunk when he came to see Momma and liked batting her around before taking her into the bedroom. The bastard's name was Reagan, and he didn't much care for Jett, either. Jett figured it was because he was always in the way whenever he wanted to be alone with Momma.

One cold winter night, Reagan locked Jett in the cellar. He wanted to drink and have a party with Momma and didn't want anyone else around. Momma didn't like that, but she put up with it because she wanted Reagan to take care of her. But one time Momma got mad at Reagan—so mad that she locked him out of her bedroom.

156

Reagan stayed away for a while—probably because he was waiting for Momma to cool off. Momma eventually cooled off, but it took a while. Meanwhile, she decided to teach Reagan a lesson. She started treating Reagan bad and giving him some only when she felt like it.

Reagan eventually evened up the score, big-time. It happened while Momma was away at the sweatshop during her bad spell, when she'd become too whiskey-stupid to attract enough men to make the rent.

Reagan, using the same soft, gentle voice he used on Momma, coaxed little twelve-year-old Jett out of his bedroom, put an arm around Jett's shoulders and took him to the head of the stairs. Reagan told Jett that they were gonna have fun at the amusement park. They had all sorts of fun games there, stuff the two of them could do together.

Jett imagined all sorts of fun games he'd be doing with Reagan and found that he was really excited about the prospect of having fun with the man. He looked up at Reagan and was about to tell the dude how much he liked being with him.

Just then, Reagan gave the boy a mighty shove, sending him sailing down the stairs. Jett flew more than halfway down, dropping hard and flipping over before hitting his head on the last four steps. A giant explosion of sizzling whiteness consumed him. A jolt of angry pain raced up his spine. Bright sparklers went off, and flames of agonizing pain engulfed him. When he landed, everything settled into a soft, gray-black haze.

When the haze finally cleared, Jett opened his eyes.

Reagan's grinning face hovered over him, his whiskey-breath a miasmic cloud brushing Jett's face. The man's grin was totally different. It wasn't like before, when he'd coaxed the boy out of his room. White strings of saliva danced from Reagan's lips, and his eyes were cold and scary. Reagan whispered: "One word about this to your momma, you dirty little bastard, and I'll shove you down those fuckin' steps again!"

Now, as Jett lay on the floor, the sparklers dancing in his head, he realized that Reagan had made good his threat.

He was coming back to push Jett down the stairs again.

Chapter 26 - 12:00 P.M.

While squeezing through a thick tangle of underbrush, Bobbie snagged her pullover on a strand of barbed wire.

Gasping at the tingling pain in her side, she spun around and gingerly began working on the material that had got hung up in the metal barbs. After pulling it free, she hiked it up.

Sure enough, the barbs had punctured her skin around the rib area, forming two jagged parallel lines about three inches long. Blood had bubbled out of the slits, but the wound wasn't deep. She pushed her top down, bent, raised a leg and squeezed between the loose strands of wire. For the next twenty yards or so, she elbowed through the thick brush, avoiding cow patties and holes in the hilly terrain. After stepping over a deadfall, she scurried down another hill. A hundred yards farther down, she reached a clearing.

A short, squat man in bib overalls stretched over his broad belly stood in front of a large gray barn, watching her. A battered conductor's cap sat on the top of his head. A double-barreled shotgun was gripped in his hands.

It was aimed in her direction.

Chapter 27 - 12:15 P.M.

Ice consulted his watch and groaned.

Damn. The Man was probably having a bird about this. Well, he'd just have to wait a few more minutes. It would have helped if he'd told Ice how sneaky this woman was...

He turned and began carefully inspecting the dump.

Someone had been here, all right. The stuff in the boxes had been disturbed, and recently. A wad of bed sheeting had been pulled out and ripped, then left lying in the weeds.

He picked up the crowbar he'd found in the grass and studied it, wondering why it wasn't rusty. This area saw a shitload of rainfall. The crowbar showed only the faintest bit of rust gathered around the claw and the other end.

Was this what she'd used on the kid? How else could she have done him in so quickly? She'd no doubt found it in the attic, used it on him, brought it with her—

Then *tossed* it?

He gazed at the hill. Why in hell would she toss a weapon as effective as a crowbar? Especially when she knew he was coming after her?

Ice lit a cigarette. Something began picking at his brain. He moved a little to his right so he could scan the hill at a different angle. From here he could see much better—the way the grass mashed down just a few feet from the crest, going down in a

160

curved pattern, toward the dump. It looked like something had rolled down the hill...

She'd obviously tripped and dropped the crowbar when she went down the hill. She might have hit her head on the way down or had the breath knocked out of her, and when she came to, she forgot all about the crowbar.

He wondered if she'd twisted an ankle. A fall like that might have done some damage. He hoped so. This was getting old. She needed to be whacked before she found someone and spilled her guts.

The only place in this area was that farm about two miles from the main road. It was run by a fat, middle-aged hayseed living with his momma. There was no security there, but if she found the place and had time to get to a phone, Ice would have to kill one fat farmer and his momma to make this right.

***

"Yer trespassin'."

The portly farmer spat out a shiny golden burst of tobacco and used the sleeve of his plaid shirt to wipe his mouth. "Got signs posted all over."

Bobbie approached him slowly, nervously eyeing the shotgun. She kept her arms at her sides. She didn't want him to think she had a weapon. "I'm truly sorry to be on your land, but I desperately need help." It was difficult staying calm, speaking coherently. "Could you...I mean, is there any chance you might have a phone?"

He spat out another shiny golden-brown ribbon and watched her.

Feeling uneasy, Bobbie thought of the flick, *Deliverance*, and wondered if the man kept pigs and

161

did nasty things with them. She immediately felt ridiculous for thinking such absurd thoughts. She needed to start thinking clearly if she wanted to get out of this.

The farmer spoke. "Got no phone."

Bobbie's heart sank. She'd hoped he could sense her urgency. She looked a mess and obviously didn't belong out here. She took a few more steps in his direction. "Do you have a car? A truck? Could you please take me into town? Is Finley close?" She tried to ignore his wandering eyes. Right now, they were focused on her pullover. She glanced down; it had hiked up an inch or two, probably when she was squeezing through the fence. She pushed it back down over her jeans. "I could pay you." She tried her best to sound earnest. "I've got some money. If I could get to a bank, I could—"

"Got a truck." He turned, and another glossy brown ribbon leaped from his mouth. "Ain't in good shape, but still gits me round."

Bobbie felt her spirits lifting. "Listen, I could—"

"Every once in a while, take 'er to town, have Herschel take a peek under the hood, git 'er runnin' again."

"Please—"

"Truck's more'n twenty, seen better days— know what I mean?"

She could feel him taking her in as he talked. His eyes stayed on her hair for a while. She could only imagine how dirty and scraggly it looked. He was probably trying to figure out why she was

162

wandering around, miles from nowhere, looking like she'd been playing in the dirt.

If only he'd let her talk...

"If you could just—"

"Could take ya in to Finley," he said suddenly, lowering the shotgun. "How 'bout I take ya in, leave ya with the sharf?" He shrugged. "All the town's got. Belmont County's a perty good size, but they only got a sharf and two depities. Sharf, far department, and post office. S'about it."

Bobbie began feeling much better. At least he wanted to help... "That would be fine, thank you. You see, my boss brought me out here, and something really horrible happened—"

"Cyrus is the big man." He either didn't hear her or wasn't paying attention. "Boy's been sharf so long, gonna get hisself buried in his uniform duds." He chuckled. "Yup. Cyrus'll take care of ya. Closest hospital's in Wheeling—"

"No, no." Bobbie was smiling with wet eyes. The warm relief rushing through her had made her knees weak. "The Sheriff will be just fine." Now that he'd lowered the shotgun, stopped rambling, and expressed an interest in helping her, everything began coming out in a torrent. "I've been running and hiding...so *long* now... This man...he's after me... He killed my boss... He's...being *paid*...I didn't *want* to come out here, but...I've got to find help..."

Her head felt hot; she reached up and rubbed her forehead. She knew she was ranting but just couldn't help it. She had to get everything out so

163

this man could understand what was going on. "Listen, I really appreciate—I could pay you—"

He turned toward the barn and the white-shingled farmhouse beyond it. He started walking up the dirt road. "Don't need no money fer helpin' out somebody that needs it."

"But I'd *like* to." She caught up to him, surprised at his oddly brisk pace. The man was built like a barrel, no more than five-eight and probably close to three hundred pounds. "I appreciate your kindness. Please let me help if I can."

"Don't take no money fer helpin' folks out. 'Specially when a body's got troubles. Good Book says so." He turned away and spat out another sleek brown squirt. "Hungry?" He gave her a quick glance, pointing his tiny brown eyes at her tiny waist.

Her stomach replied in its own crude way, reminding her of how long it had been since she'd last eaten. Then she remembered how close her pursuer could be. She risked a quick glance behind them but saw nothing but beautiful pastureland.

"I haven't eaten in…quite a while, but I really can't stay—"

"Cain't have *that*." He shook his head. "Momma'd skin me alive, she knew I let a body leave the place hungry. 'Specially a gal skinny as you." He raised both bushy brows. "Like stuff cabbage?"

"*Love* it." Her mouth watered.

They passed the barn. Two Quarter Horse mares watched from their paddock on one side of the barn. The larger of the two followed, stopping at the corner of the fence and nibbling on the hay sticking out of her mouth.

The house was well-used and cluttered. The kitchen was warm and had that rich food-smell that made Bobbie's mouth water as soon as the man pulled open the ancient screen door. However, she was extremely reluctant to relax in such a warm, comfy place with a murderer so frighteningly close. But now she had an ally and at least the illusion of safety. And the man had mentioned his mother. She imagined a gutsy, gun-toting Ma Barker and felt strangely relaxed.

Also, the farmer had a shotgun. Would the murdering bastard risk coming here and taking her in front of a witness? In front of *two* witnesses?

"Set yourself down," he said, disappearing to another room. "Take just a sec to fix." He returned to the kitchen empty-handed.

Bobbie was surprised to find a wooden chair with a taped-up vinyl pad so comfortable. "You live here with your mother?" She couldn't stop staring at the screen door.

He went to the stove, grabbed a stained red-and-white checked potholder from a hook on the wall and lifted the heavy metal lid off the tarnished steel pot. He winced as the billowing steam escaped, hitting him in the face before fanning outwards, toward the peeled plaster ceiling. "Yup. 'S'been her place the last sixty years."

The sweet-sour smell of stuffed cabbage filled the room. Bobbie closed her eyes and thought she'd died and gone to heaven. "Where's your mom?" She tried to peer around the corner. She wanted to see the old lady sitting in a rocker, cleaning a large-caliber revolver.

The farmer found a large green bowl from the cupboard and put it on the stove. "Stayin' with her sister the weekend, up near Flushing. Ma's always got somethin goin' on with Aint Tess."

Damn. Just the two of them...

No. I can't stay here. The panic bubbled up, and she practically jumped up from the chair. "Please...we really need to leave...right now...I appreciate your kindness, but—"

"It's all right."

"But—"

"Don't let it worry ya none." He was grinning.

"You just don't understand—"

"Momma won't mind. Like I said, she wouldn't want ya leavin' the place hungry." He turned, his chubby face in a lopsided grin. "'Sides, there's 'nuff cabbage here fer—" He stopped abruptly and his grin quickly dissolved. The stainless-steel spoon slid from his grasp, its shiny hook catching on his thumb, dangling over the scuffed linoleum. Brown-red sauce dripped in thick gobs on the scuffed floor. His gaze had slipped from Bobbie to the screen door, which groaned loudly.

Bobbie turned sharply.

He was standing in the doorway, an obscene grin on his rough features, his insane blue-gray eyes fixed on her.

A large sizzling-hot coal filled Bobbie's gut. She found that she couldn't move or even breathe.

Her luck had finally run out.

166

Chapter 28 - 12:30 P.M.

Ice crossed the room in three quick strides and stopped just a couple of feet from the girl.

She was the one, all right. But right now she was a far cry from the photo the Man had sent on his phone. Her hair was sloppy and filled with briars and bits of grass, her makeup runny and her big, dark-brown eyes bloodshot. Dirt and sweat smudged her forehead, and she'd begun to smell bad.

She'd apparently stumbled here and asked Farmer Boy for help. What else would a fathead like Elmer Fudd be doing with such a hot number? The fat fuck had no doubt been doing hand-jobs in the shitter the last forty years and wouldn't have any idea what to do with a genuine babe.

She stood shivering at the table, her eyes ready to pop out of the sockets. The grass stains on her jeans made his pulse hammer. So did the big, jagged gash on the side of her pullover, exposing her pink flesh. Even filthy, she was a hot-looking dish.

Fat Boy stood in front of the stove—a quivering mass of gooey custard, the bibs keeping the soft stuff from splashing the linoleum.

"Somethin' smells awfully tasty in here," Ice said amiably. "Stuffed cabbage?" He sniffed, his enormous chest rising. "Wish I could oblige, old man, but this cutie'n me…well, we've got serious business back at the house."

She shifted her weight and tried moving away.

Ice grabbed her by the wrist, pulling her against him and twisting her arm sharply behind her, tearing a squeal of pain out of her throat. He positioned her wrist, pulling up her arm so her hand was just a few inches from her neck.

She felt nice against him—warm and juicy. Her sweat smelled sweet.

He turned to Fat Boy. "I've been lookin' for this lady for quite a while. Thanks for findin' her for me."

The farmer didn't speak. Still trembling, he'd lowered his gaze to the floor. His large head turned briefly toward the next room, making Ice wonder if the farmer kept a shotgun. It only stood to reason. These farm boys always had something in the house for stray dogs, deer, coyotes, coons, snakes... Ice didn't think there would be a problem. Fat Boy was too busy shitting his drawers to try anything.

Ice thought of Elmer Fudd from those old cartoons. He wanted to hear the fat fool say "wascally wabbit." It would be a real kick.

Ice loved fun games. While he had Gina staked out naked in the woods, he'd played the "this little piggy" game, breaking each finger, one at a time, before moving on to the toes.

It would be great fun killing Elmer, here. He just couldn't devote as much time to it as he would have liked. He was behind schedule as it was.

But five extra minutes wouldn't make *that* much of a difference, would it?

Still holding on to the girl's arm, Ice dragged her over to where the farmer was standing. When he

168

was just a foot away he looked down at him and said, "Any questions, Elmer?"

The farmer shook his head.

"This is between me and her—got it?"

The girl muttered something, but Ice jerked her pinned arm upward, making her whimper.

The farmer winced.

"Good. Now that we understand one another, got any empty feed sacks?"

The farmer didn't reply.

"Don't make me ask you again, now..."

The farmer nodded.

"We're gonna have a little party—got it?"

The farmer kept gazing at the floor. He obviously didn't want to look at the girl's taut white face.

"Let's go get 'em, then. And I'm gonna need your truck for a little while."

***

As the sparklers kept going off, Jett groped for the doorway.

He took a deep breath and stretched until he felt the hard, angled wood filling his palm. Then, tilting his head, he reached out with his other hand.

Something was blocking him but reluctantly slid away. He reached out and examined it. It felt like a chair lying on its side. He wondered why a chair would be lying on its side in a doorway. All that mattered was that it was in his way, so he gritted his teeth and shoved it to the side.

He began groping for the other side of the doorway. Once he found it, he grasped it and held on tightly. Then, lowering his head to the floor, he held his breath and pulled.

A penetrating knot of pain stabbed him between the shoulder blades. He clenched his jaw until it hurt, his neck muscles standing out like quivering harp strings beneath his flushed skin. To his amazement, he felt himself sliding out into the hall.

Reagan, you mean bastard, you're gonna have your hands full this time.

I ain't goin' down those stairs ever again!

Chapter 29 - 12:45 P.M.

Shaking violently, Farmer Boy stood with his huge ass mashed against the wooden wall of the hayloft.

Giant dark circles of sweat showed under his flabby, plaid-covered arms. He'd been standing like this since Ice had brought him inside for twine and a burlap sack.

The fear showed in the man's quivering chins, his bloated cheeks glistening sweat, his swollen belly trembling like Jell-O beneath the dirty bibs, the dark stain covering his denim crotch and in the loud stomach sounds from the plug of tobacco he'd accidentally swallowed on the way to the barn.

Ice grabbed the pitchfork leaning against the wooden beam near the wall of the loft. "Looks like you're gonna have one of those, uh, freak accidents, Elmer," he said softly, almost to himself.

The farmer found his voice. "Pl-Please...d-d-don't hurt me, M-Mister!" His pudgy fingers clawed at the splintered wall.

Ice hated to see a grown man turning into a quivering, spineless mess. He really couldn't blame him. Out here, the only excitement Elmer got was probably a stray dog pissing off the horses, or a fox feasting on one of the chickens. This was big-time, and he just couldn't handle it. He'd stood idly by just a few minutes ago, too petrified to move, as Ice taped up the girl, stuck the burlap sack over her head, picked her up, flung her over his shoulder and carried her outside.

"I ain't gonna hurt you, Elmer." Ice lowered the pitchfork and thumped the round end of the long handle on the wooden floor between their feet. He brought the four rusty tines into view, resting the two middle ones gently against the farmer's soft chins. "We're just gonna have a little fun, is all."

The farmer stood stock-still, the jagged points pinching his sagging flesh. He gingerly lifted his head. Ice raised the fork, and the tines continued pressing against the man's soft, glimmering flesh.

Ice moved closer. The smile on his face was gone. "Listen, Elmer... I want you to say 'wascally wabbit,' five times in a row, as fast as you can."

The terrified man gulped audibly. His eyes were no longer focused. The brown centers twitched, and his entire body shivered.

"C'mon, dickhead." Ice was getting impatient. "Say it."

The fat man gulped again. "Pl-Pl-Please..."

"*Say* it, dammit." The tines jerked upwards.

The farmer's sweat-covered face turned chalky-white. His eyes glazed over. "B-B-But—"

"*Say* it, you fat pile of shit."

The man's face turned bright red.

The tines jerked up two more inches, drawing a harsh gasp from the terrified man. Blood eased down the rusty sides of the twines slowly, like syrup.

"One last chance, fat boy..." Ice licked his lips and felt the beginnings of a hard-on.

The fear...it was so lovely... The ultimate turn-on...

The farmer stood up on tiptoe and tried turning his head. Desperate, he finally found the courage to reach out for the pitchfork.

"Stupid bastard." Ice rammed it all the way up, until the tines completely disappeared in the soft flesh of the farmer's jowls.

The man's twitching eyes filled the sockets. His arms jerked like the limbs of a dancing marionette. His hands began waving uselessly in front of him. It looked like he'd just eaten something too hot. His jaw dropped; his mouth fell open. A gurgling sound escaped his throat. One of the blood-covered tines was visible, puncturing the roof of the man's mouth. Blood spurted outwards, streaking his bibs, and flowing down his bloated gut.

The farmer's body shook. A strangled cry erupted from his gaping mouth. His hands waved another second or two before dropping limply to his sides. His eyes glazed over. His knees gave out, but the pitchfork prevented him from going all the way down. It forced his head back, and he gazed unseeingly at the rafters.

Ice kicked the pitchfork away, snapping the man's neck. In one last heavy splash of blood, the farmer fell and lay on his side, legs and arms twitching, until he no longer moved.

Ice stood there another minute or so. Then he caught a whiff of the stuffed cabbage flowing in from the direction of the kitchen. His gut protested loudly. "Know somethin', Elmer? You just made me work up an appetite. I think I'm gonna have to sample that cabbage after all."

173

On his way back to the house, he pulled out his cell, pressed the number and sent the following text: *EVERYTHING READY. BOTH PACKAGES PICKED UP AND READY TO BE SENT.*

There. That should make the big guy feel better. The hundred and twenty-five K would be in Ice's account by next morning.

Ice pulled the sim card from the cell, dropped the cell on the ground, smashed it with his boot, picked up the pieces and tossed them into the bushes. He'd toss the sim card on the way back. He glanced at the pickup, where he'd dumped the chick. She was still moving around in the bed but hadn't gone anywhere.

It would only take him a few minutes to grab a helping or two of that stuffed cabbage. It sure smelled good.

Farmers were boneheads, but they really knew how to cook.

***

Enveloped in darkness, Jett managed to crawl over to some sort of contraption in the middle of the black tunnel.

It felt like a ladder...

He examined it with the fingers of his right hand. He experienced a flicker of memory and wondered if he'd brought it here...or if someone else had done it...

Now he wasn't so sure. He couldn't even remember why he'd brought a ladder into this tunnel.

Another glimmer flared in the darkness—a basement, a furnace, a coal bin. Just before

174

confusion set in, he experienced another flash—this time, the attic staircase...

Yes. That was it. He'd been looking for something, and the moment he tried remembering, the basement flickered in his head once again. Someone had been hiding down there, so terrified that she wouldn't come out.

She? Momma?

It came trickling back. Momma had gone down into the basement to hide from Reagan so he wouldn't find her and slap her around, as he always did whenever he came to the house drunk.

Jett looked up. At first, he saw nothing but more darkness...but when he squinted and tilted his head just a tad to the left, he saw the dark, hazy blur of the staircase.

But why was it lowered?

Momma had obviously lowered it. When she was convinced Reagan had left, she'd come out of the basement and snuck up to the attic. Now that the coast was clear, Jett had to help get her down.

"Momma?" He kept his voice soft, so Reagan wouldn't hear—just in case the bastard hadn't really left. "You up there?"

Silence. Had she already come back down?

If Momma had come back down, it was because Reagan had conned her down. Reagan was good at conning people to do things. He'd conned Momma into doing a lot of things she hadn't wanted to do. Hell, the bastard had conned Jett out of his room just to push him down the stairs.

Reagan hadn't had much trouble conning Momma. It usually only took a fancy dinner and a movie, where she could dress up and look really nice. Momma was at her happiest when everyone was looking at her and making her feel better about herself.

Maybe Momma wasn't hiding in the attic or the basement. Maybe she and Reagan had gone out. When they came back later on, they'd have drinks and head right off to bed, and Jett wouldn't see her again until the next morning.

This time, he suspected, Reagan would wait until Momma was asleep before he got out of bed and went to look for Jett.

The attic staircase...

Now it could be used for something else.

Chapter 30 - 1:15 P.M.

Frozen terror sliced through Bobbie as she bounced around in the bed of the farmer's truck.

However, she could not scream. The big brute had stuffed a dirty rag in her mouth and then slapped a strip of duct tape over her lips from a small roll he'd taken out of his jacket pocket. He used the tape to secure her wrists together behind her back, then pulled a heavy burlap feed sack over her head and fastened it around her waist with baling twine he'd got from stacks of hay piled on palettes in a corner of the barn. Once he'd fixed her up properly, he led her outside, set her on the open tailgate of the farmer's truck, taped her ankles together, shoved her inside the bed and slammed the tailgate shut.

While she lay there, bound and helpless, he went back to the barn. She heard shouting, then silence. Then, after another minute or two, a horrible shriek just before something slammed against the wall of the barn.

Moments later, she heard his footsteps. They were heavy and quick, and sounded like he was walking back to the house.

About five minutes later, the screen door slammed shut and she heard his footsteps once again. They moved much quicker this time and grew louder as he approached the truck.

Before sliding into the cab, he belched loudly and chuckled. "Elmer was a fat butthole, but he sure knew how to make stuffed cabbage." He opened the door and climbed in. When he slammed the door shut, the truck shook on its ancient springs.

Bobbie bit down so hard on the wet rag, it made her jaws ache.

That monster just killed an innocent man—did he have to go inside and help himself to the poor man's dinner?

She began thinking of her penknife, which sat comfortably in her front pocket.

If only she could get her hands on it...

***

Crawling on the floor, Jett tried to tell himself that the throbbing pain in his head would eventually go away.

It was easy to ignore pain and most other things while he was thinking of Reagan. He could even ignore the fact that he could hardly see. A thick wall of darkness had been hovering in front of him. To make matters worse, the sparklers continued going off in his head. They seemed pretty far away most of the time, but when the throbbing increased, they grew much brighter. But that wasn't important right now. It sure was tough going when you had to squint to see past a solid wall of darkness.

As he crawled, the throbbing in his head increased dramatically. He wanted to cover his ears but needed his hands to push himself toward the doorway. He had to make it to safety. Once Momma and Reagan were finished in the bedroom, Momma would put on her nightie and walk barefoot into the kitchen to fix drinks. And while Momma was busy, Reagan would come upstairs looking for Jett.

178

No more, Jett thought angrily, forcing the fear away. *You're not gonna play your games with me again. You can't play your games if you can't find me.*

With a mighty heave, he pushed himself forward, veering left, where the bottom step would be.

***

Ignoring the pain in her shoulders and hips, Bobbie pulled her bound wrists toward her right pocket.

Unfortunately for her, he'd tied the open end of the burlap sack shut around her waist. In doing so, he'd hidden her taped wrists from view, but also made it nearly impossible for her to reach her pocket. There was some slack in the twine, but she'd have to struggle considerably to slip her bound wrists through the opening to get to the pocket. To make things even more difficult, she had to keep her right side out of his range of vision—which was difficult while rolling around in a moving truck. But there was no other alternative, and she knew it wouldn't be long before he'd be getting out of the truck. She had no way of knowing how long the return trip would take but assumed that it couldn't be very long. However, it felt like an eternity, as evidenced by the pain in her knees, hips and lower back. Not to mention the throbbing fire in both shoulders and her right arm and wrist from when he'd manhandled her in the farmhouse.

Forcing herself to focus, she tensed her cramped arms and made another mighty effort to force her bound wrists closer to her pocket.

Ice kept the old truck at thirty-five despite the posted signs that said twenty.

Some signs even posted ten for the horseshoe bends. He kept his eye on the rearview and watched the delicious bundle bouncing around in the bed of the truck like a sack of loose rocks.

"Not much longer, baby," he muttered, grinning. He took the next sharp bend much faster than necessary, jerking the wheel and making her slam into the tire well.

Later, as he drove down a straight stretch, with barbed wire spanning both sides of the roadway, he tossed the sim card into the brush just off the shoulder. Then, glancing in the rearview, he noticed her cramping up a little and twisting to her right. She'd probably pulled a muscle. This was no big deal. A pulled muscle wouldn't make much difference. In half an hour, she wouldn't be feeling much of anything anymore.

He inhaled some Marlboro and pushed it right back out. "Make that forty-five minutes," he said, thinking of those fine tits bouncing around inside that pullover.

***

Jett heaved his body up until the bottom step of the attic staircase supported his weight.

When he looked straight up, he thought he saw a flash of something bright. He closed his eyes tight. He wanted to rub them but needed both hands to hold on to the step. A heavy wave of nausea swept through him when the staircase swayed just a little.

180

He couldn't stop now; he had to get up there and hide.

Hiding was his only chance. Hiding and waiting.

Another bright flash raced across his vision, and a series of soft crunching sounds went on inside his head. It sounded almost like stitching being torn loose from a shirt, or duct tape being ripped from a roll.

Wincing, he felt a swarm of hotness in the back of his head. It began moving downwards to the base of his neck.

"Hurts…" He gritted his teeth while pulling himself up the staircase. "It *really* hurts…"

Chapter 31 - 1:45 P.M.

Ice pulled the truck up the narrow dirt road, parked behind the silver Porsche, and switched off the ignition.

The truck coughed quietly into silence. When he kicked open the door, it swung out with a tired groan. He climbed down and went to the back, dropping the tailgate with a loud *thunk* that made the vehicle rock on its frame. He bent and, resting his gut against the tailgate, reached for the bundle.

She pulled away.

Growling, he wrapped his right hand tightly around a taped ankle and yanked hard, driving a gasp from her. When both ankles reached the tailgate she offered some resistance again, but only briefly.

"Don't piss me off, bitch." He jabbed her behind the left ankle with his thumb, driving a muffled shriek from her. "I might just strangle ya right here."

Once she lay still, he grabbed the burlap sack by the twine and made her sit on the tailgate. Using his hunting knife, he began slicing through the tape securing her ankles together. "I need ya to walk." He freed her ankles and pulled her into a standing position. "At least, for now."

He grabbed her upper arm tightly and led her to the front steps of the house, then stopped abruptly. "Careful. I don't want ya breakin' your neck before we start partyin'." Then he led her up the front steps.

***

Using the last of his strength, Jett heaved himself into the attic opening and rolled onto the plywood sheeting.

More fireworks flared up in the darkness of his head. He lay there, gasping for breath. Then he suddenly remembered a friend who'd hidden in an attic. He tried to recall his friend's name but couldn't. He closed his eyes and concentrated, but the sparklers went off again and the throbbing started back up. He found that he couldn't even remember what his friend looked like. He wondered if he'd just imagined it...or maybe he was just remembering some old movie he'd seen...

Yeah. It was an old movie—something about a little girl hiding in an attic during World War II. She couldn't have been much more than Jett's age, possibly a few years younger. She was hiding with a bunch of other people while the Nazis were running around, looking for Jews to round up and stick in concentration camps.

He remembered watching it one rainy Saturday afternoon. Momma was sitting in the chair next to him, not saying much because she was in one of her dark moods.

He also remembered some lady hiding in a cellar, and a friend who'd come to work on someone's barn. Jett's friend—this big, strong guy with a shaved head and tattoos—was gonna give him money so Jett could get Momma away from the sweatshop, where she'd been working. And it would

183

help her get away from Reagan, who liked doing bad things to Momma and Jett...

Just then, Jett heard the roar of a truck outside. His heart skipped a beat, and he froze.

It was Reagan. Jett recognized the sound of the bastard's old truck. The way it backfired after Reagan switched off the engine...the loud groaning sound the door made when Reagan kicked it open.

Jett squinted his eyes shut and rubbed his temples. He needed a clear head right now. It had to be clear enough to do what needed to be done.

***

Ice led the girl into the living room and pushed her down in the armchair.

He stood there tensely, watching her. Those long legs were doing a serious number on him, and he knew right then that he was going to do what he wanted with her before he smothered her and set fire to the house. He couldn't let such prime stuff get by without a little poking first.

He decided to take her upstairs and do her properly in the bed. He wanted her stripped naked and spread-eagled. He liked them stretched out so he could watch them squirm and buck. He wanted to see those long legs pulling and kicking. It made his blood boil. In his view, there was nothing hotter.

"Get up." He reached out for the front of the sack. Then, gripping the thick burlap, he gave it a yank, until she was on her feet again. She grunted but managed to stay on her feet.

He moved his face closer. He could hear her breath coming out of her nostrils in short, quick

184

gasps. It heated him up even more. "Party time," he whispered. Then he led her over to the staircase.

***

Reagan and Momma were coming up the stairs.

They climbed the steps slowly, one at a time, and Jett could hear the bastard chuckling as they approached the landing. He wanted to peek out through the opening but didn't want to give away his position. With Reagan, you had to try and catch him off-guard. Reagan was a sly fox and seemed to sense things before they happened. It had something to do with him spending some time in prison. He'd once told Jett that when you were in prison, you had to sleep with one eye open, and you never turned your back on anyone, or you'd get shivved in the back.

Even so, Jett was confident that he might be able to catch the bastard off guard. Jett was really messed up. He could hardly see, his head wouldn't stop throbbing, and the sparklers kept going off. But one thing stayed with him as he sat there, just a foot or so from the attic opening.

Reagan, if you want me, you're gonna have to climb these stairs...

***

The moment the two of them reached the top step, the big brute snatched Bobbie by the arm and stopped cold.

For long, agonizing moments, he didn't move. Bobbie was afraid of moving for fear of enraging him. She wondered if he was considering which room to take her. Or maybe he was looking at the boy. She shivered, knowing that the sight of his

185

friend lying there dead or unconscious would probably get him thinking of what horrible things he was going to do to her before he killed her.

Finally, he led her into a room and stopped abruptly. Once again, they just stood there. Bobbie began shivering even worse. She could tell he was considering what he was going to do next. She had to lock her knees so they wouldn't give way. She told herself she could not faint…that he'd probably rape her anyway if she did.

I will not faint, she promised herself. *I won't give him the satisfaction.*

"On the bed." He backed her up against it and pushed her down. "And you'd better not move…"

The blood thundered icily through Bobbie's veins as she sat on the soft mattress, waiting. After about a minute, she thought she heard quiet footsteps outside the room. She waited, wondering what was going to happen. Then it dawned on her.

He wasn't even in the room…

What on earth was happening?

***

There was no sign of the kid.

Ice moved silently into the hall. He stood stock-still, listening for the slightest sound. He gazed at the stepladder, then the attic opening. He took three quiet steps and regarded the staircase and the landing below, listening intensely to the silence. The wooden chair still lay on its side, just a couple of feet from the bedroom doorway…

But it looked like it had been pushed to the side.

If the kid came to, where had he gone?

186

He crept silently into the room and looked around, peering around the corner. Other than the stiff lying on the bed, the room was empty. He got down on hands and knees and pushed up a portion of the bedspread. A black leather shoulder bag and denim jacket lay underneath. He pulled them out. Carrying them, he crossed the room and went back to the other room, where the girl sat on the edge of the bed, still encased in the burlap sack. He dropped the jacket on her lap, startling her. Then he slammed the bag down beside her on the mattress, startling her again.

He forced himself not to belt her. He'd save that for later, when he'd removed the sack. It wasn't much fun when they couldn't see what you were going to do. He scooped up the jacket and the bag and tossed them both. The bag opened, spilling its contents.

A sourness moved sluggishly up his throat. She'd obviously been hiding under the bed while Ice in the attic. She was under the damn bed in the next room, waiting to ambush the poor kid. "Clever, ain'tcha?" He gave the shivering bundle an irritated glare. "No wonder you could brain the kid."

Just then, he heard something out in the hall.

He pulled the revolver from his waistband and tiptoed silently out of the room.

**

As Jett shifted his position, his foot thumped against something.

He'd obviously knocked something over. It rolled on the plywood sheeting and bumped against something else. He groped for it and picked it up.

It was smooth, warm.

A glass. Maybe a jar...

He squinted, trying to see it better. He couldn't see much of anything, so he brought it closer to his ear. It sounded like liquid sloshing around. He tried sniffing it, but his sniffer had quit working, too. He smelled only the mustiness of the attic and something foul—something he didn't want to think about right now.

He put the jar down, moved closer to the attic opening and listened. Then he heard something and felt a rush of warmth in his crotch, and another whiff of that same sour stench.

Reagan was down there, looking for him.

***

Ice checked out the landing but found nothing.

But it sure sounded like that thump had come from out here. Maybe the kid crawled to another room to rest. He'd been really freaked out about the stiff in the other room.

Ice walked over and cracked open the door. He paused a moment before shoving it open. "Kid? You in here?" He dropped to his knees and checked beneath the bed. Once again, there was nothing. He straightened and hurried out of the room. He had visions of Jett wandering around like one of those stupid zombies in that classic old flick, *Night of the Living Dead*, not knowing his name, where he was or what happened. "Kid, where the fuck are ya?"

Strangely, he felt better, knowing Jett had come to. The kid was a pain, but good to have around. He could be wandering around the house, trying to get his nut back.

188

Ice grinned when the idea came to him.

Let the kid have the bitch first...

It made sense. The kid would no doubt enjoy getting his hands on the bitch who'd planted the knot on his skull. He'd probably love fucking her while she was staked out on the bed.

It would benefit both of them. Ice would enjoy standing close by, watching.

"Kid, where are ya? Wanna play a really fun game?"

189

Chapter 32 - 2:00 P.M.

Shivering in fear, Bobbie struggled to get the blade out of the knife handle.

It was quite an effort. The handle was less than three inches long and difficult to hold. Her taped wrists fought her every inch of the way, but after getting a good, tight grip on the handle, she worked furiously.

In the midst of her efforts, her thumbnail peeled backwards, and she squealed in agony, biting down hard on the cloth in her mouth. Tears filled her eyes.

Seconds later, she heard the big brute calling for someone out in the hall.

The boy…he was still alive?

It made sense. She'd pulled back at the last second, hadn't she? She couldn't force herself to kill a defenseless boy, even if it meant the difference between life and death.

Although the knowledge somehow made her feel better, she fully understood the frightening downside of her compassionate effort.

If that boy ever gets his hands on me…

***

Jett pulled himself into a sitting position near the attic opening.

All he could see were gooey splashes of gray and brown. He could smell something burning. But even though his hearing was a little distorted, he could tell by the sound of Reagan's voice that the bastard wasn't very far away.

Momma was probably taking a bath and getting herself all prettied-up. Jett knew he couldn't rely on her. He'd already tried telling her what the man had done. It had taken him a while to gather the courage, to convince himself he hadn't been the one at fault, but when he finally got it out, Momma immediately confronted the bastard.

It turned out to be a horrible mistake.

Half-drunk, Reagan had dragged Momma into the bedroom for one of their worst shouting matches ever. Terrified, Jett locked himself in his bedroom and hid under the bed. Even so, Jett could hear Momma screaming and crying, then the sounds of slapping, of things being knocked to the floor and slammed against the wall. When Momma came out later on, her mouth was covered with bloody splotches. Her mouth was so swollen, she could hardly talk.

Reagan had followed her out of the bedroom and was ready to kick even more ass. The wild look in the bastard's eyes reminded Jett of one of those werewolf flicks he'd seen on TV a few weeks earlier. While Momma was cleaning up in the bathroom, Reagan pulled Jett roughly aside and whispered: "You're next, you stupid son of a whore..."

Momma barricaded herself in the cellar right afterward, biding her time until Reagan got tired of yelling and banging on the cellar door. After a while, Reagan finally settled down. Tired from the yelling and from the beating he'd given Momma, he'd chugged down a couple of quick beers. Then, feeling somewhat mellow, he left.

Jett had gone down to the cellar later on and found Momma hiding in the coal bin. He helped her upstairs and got her a warm washcloth for her bruises and cuts. At the time, he had no idea that even though Reagan had beaten her bloody, the bastard would get back into her good graces later on, when he told her how sorry he was and that he wouldn't have done any of that if he hadn't been drunk. He'd even told her that pushing Jett down the stairs was an accident.

Momma not only believed him, but she'd also gone out with him again.

A soft growl coming from his throat, Jett positioned his feet on the third step of the attic staircase.

C'mon, you bastard...

We'll play a fun game you'll never forget...

***

After inspecting another bedroom, Ice hurried back to the master and looked in.

She was sitting on the bed as before. She'd shifted a little, but he could tell she hadn't tried anything stupid. One look at the shapely figure and Ice felt the twang of an erection. "Not much longer," he whispered, licking his lips. Then he turned and glanced at the attic opening.

The boy was up there, his head cocked at a weird angle. His tennis shoes rested on the third step. The kid looked like he was about to jump.

"Hey, kid." He moved closer. "What the hell ya doin' up there?"

Silence. Jett was gazing in Ice's direction, but there was a spooky expression on his face. He was squinting. Ice wondered just how badly the woman had hurt him.

"C'mon down." He tucked the gun in his waistband and took another step toward the staircase. "What the hell ya doin' sittin' there like that?"

"You know damn well what I'm doin'." The kid sounded angry.

Ice cocked his head. The boy obviously wasn't thinking straight. But once Ice got him down, he'd talk some sense into him and get him fixed up later on. You could buy a shitload of painkillers when you had a hundred and twenty-five grand in the kitty. The boy might even be okay when Ice helped him settle the score with the chick.

"It's gonna be all right," Ice said. "I'm back. C'mon down and we'll play a game. I wanna show ya who's in the bedroom down here—"

"Another *fun* game?"

"Howzat?"

Ice began wondering why Jett sounded so different. He didn't sound at all like himself. He sounded like he was nine or ten years old.

"Don't wanna play no *fun* games no more..."

"Dammit, kid, c'mon down. I promise you'll have lots of fun. We both will. I got the bitch that belted ya down here, all bundled up and ready for both of us—"

"Don't *wanna* play no more," the kid growled, and Ice could see the kid's skinny, dirt-covered arms tensing as he gripped the wooden frame of the attic trap.

"Listen, kid..." Ice took a deep breath. This was getting old. A lot of things had to be done and they were running out of time. At least the kid was still alive; that was one less problem to deal with. He just hoped the kid wasn't beyond reasoning. Right now, it seemed as if the boy's brains had been pounded into oatmeal. Ice hoped he was wrong. He really didn't want to finish him off. "Kid, if ya don't come down here right now, I'm comin' up after ya..."

"Don't *wanna* play your fuckin' games *no more!*" The boy's face had turned beet-red. His head twisted as he yelled.

"Have it your way, kid. I'm comin' up." Ice raised his leg and put his foot on the bottom step. The sudden burden of his weight made the staircase sway and jerk to the right.

A loud gasp escaped the boy's throat. His face suddenly lost all color. A split second later, he leaped down.

***

Jett's knees came down first, slamming into Ice's shoulders and forcing him to the floor.

Both men lay on the landing for long moments, barely moving. Then, finally, Jett rolled over on his side and began groping blindly for Ice.

Ice immediately came to, cradling his bruised shoulders and moaning softly. Hearing him, Jett crawled over. Tightening both hands around Ice's thick neck, Jett dug his thumbs savagely into Ice's throat.

Growling, Ice pounded the boy with his fists. Jett didn't seem to feel the powerful blows. The

194

kid's face had squeezed into a strange smile. His nose was wrinkled and pulled up, like a snarling animal's. His mouth was squeezed tight. Strings of saliva swayed from his lower lip.

For the first time in his life, Ice experienced genuine fear. A heavy sheet of cold slid up his spine. The kid clung to him like a fetid disease. He was mumbling about not playing any more games...that Reagan would never hurt him or his momma ever again...

Suddenly overcome with exhaustion, Ice stopped punching the boy. The kid had gone crazy and felt no pain. Like it or not, the only thing that would straighten him out was a bullet.

Gasping for breath, Ice reached between them, groping for the gun in his waistband.

Chapter 33 - 2:15 P.M.

A gunshot blast shook the walls of the house.

Bobbie gasped in terror. The inside of the burlap sack grew hotter. She froze, struggling to breathe as the intense reverberations echoed in her ears.

The silence that followed was just as deafening as the gunshot. She heard only her own heart thumping away, magnified within the confines of the sack. She was terrified of moving, of even breathing. When the silence continued, her heartbeat finally returned to normal, and a strange ringing sound filled her head. Not a sound came from the hall.

Were they dead? Had they both been killed by the blast?

She wanted to rip through the burlap with her penknife and run. But since she had no idea what faced her, she knew better. A strange voice inside her began telling her things might not be as they seemed...that she shouldn't move or make a sound.

Moments later, the thuds of heavy footsteps out in the hall grew louder as they approached the bedroom.

***

Ice staggered clumsily to the bedroom doorway and leaned against the doorframe, gasping for air.

His neck throbbed. Red welts pitted with bloody fingerprints covered the massive column of solid flesh beneath his jaw. He coughed, spat blood.

His neck was on fire. He reached up and gently felt the swollen flesh.

He'd survive this...but he was in no mood for fucking right now. In fact, the only thing he wanted was to get this business taken care of so he could collect his money and split. Without the kid's help, it was going to be rough. The original plan would go as planned, but now there would be loose ends to fix.

Right now, the woman had to be taken care of. She was probably more than ready to die anyway.

With a humorless grin, the big man eyed the bundle.

Those legs began doing a number on him again... Those long legs in the tight jeans...that pullover hiding those smooth, perky jugs...

Ice approached the helpless figure. The pain in his crotch was even more unbearable than the stabbing fire in his neck. Pain or no pain, he'd have his way with her. He wanted that smooth, silky skin between his fingers. He wanted to watch her squirm.

He could barely contain himself as he began undoing the twine holding the sack closed. "We're gonna have some fun, baby," he said with a devilish grin. He untied the sack and pulled it up. "You're a fox, all right." Ice studied her closely. The strange expression on her face told him she wasn't as scared as she should be.

Well, maybe that was all right, because she'd been through a lot. She could be in shock and might not even know what was going on.

197

He bent and got ready to pinch her nostrils shut. At that same moment he thought of Gina, and the memories made his blood boil even worse. Grinning, he closed his eyes as he fondly remembered what he'd done to her.

***

Finally freed from the smothering confines of the sack, Bobbie sucked in a huge lungful of fresh air.

The cold fear numbing her had disappeared. All that mattered right now was that she had one chance only to kill him. But this time she could not possibly pull back at the last moment.

For the first time in her life, she would have to kill a human being.

He bent and extended his right arm toward her, but at the last moment, stopped and lowered it to his knee. Then he grinned and closed his eyes. She guessed he was imagining what he was going to do to her. She knew right then that she couldn't wait any longer. It was now or never.

Seconds later, he opened his eyes.

His gaze didn't shift even when her arm appeared from behind her back. It took him several moments to see that her arm was now free…that jagged threads of tape dangled loosely from her wrist…that the tape had been sliced…and that her arms were free…

Once the realization hit him, it took him another precious second or two to notice the tiny gleaming object extending from her fist as it sailed upward, toward his face.

Bobbie's arm, fueled by fear and terror, moved upwards. She delivered the blow quickly—without thinking or pulling back. It was the only way to end the nightmare.

The three-inch-long blade of her penknife buried itself to the hilt in the man's left eyeball.

***

Whimpering quietly, Jett sat near the top step of the staircase, his trembling arms wrapped around his bloody torso as the life steadily drained from him.

The blood formed a dark pool on the wooden floor beneath him, gathering at the edge and seeping down in slender streams. His teeth chattered as his body temperature dropped.

Everything had become hazy and dark, filled with gooey shapes and images. However, he'd successfully prevented Reagan from pushing him down the stairs, and even though the bastard shot him and then went back to Momma, Jett hadn't gone down those steps.

A horrible scream exploded from the bedroom, where Reagan had gone to look for Momma.

***

The knife slapped into the soft flesh of the big man's eyeball with a disgusting wet sound.

Without a second's pause, Bobbie rolled to the other side of the bed.

Howling like a dying animal, the big man groped clumsily for the knife handle protruding grotesquely from his eye socket. Blood spurted outwards, splashing the wall, the nightstand, and the bed sheets. Warm drops slapped Bobbie's face, making her cringe. Whimpering, the brute reached for the knife. His blood-splattered fingers accidentally tapped the handle. He screamed again, his head jerking backwards, his blood-smeared face lifted, strings of red phlegm dancing from his gaping mouth and bloodstained teeth.

He tried a second time to pull the knife out, squealing loudly when he accidentally jarred the handle again. Gingerly he removed it, shrieking in agony when the blade emerged. A thick spray of gore and optic fluid thumped to the floorboards. He let the knife drop to the floor and began stumbling toward her, his right eye tightly shut, his left a swollen pulp of blood and fluids. Sobbing, he swiped his huge, blood-smeared arms weakly at empty air.

Tripping on one of Bobbie's lipstick tubes, he gasped and went down hard, his feet flying out from under him. He landed on his tailbone, his huge frame shaking the floor. For long moments he rolled helplessly in the bloody gore, crying as he fumbled for something to grab onto. He managed to grasp the footboard of the bed and hauled himself up. Then, gathering up what strength he had left, he turned in her direction and began shuffling blindly toward her.

Mindful of her scattered purse contents, Bobbie backed out of the room and made her way for the staircase.

***

Moaning softly as he sat on the floor, his jeans soaked in blood, Jett heard Momma and Reagan coming out of the bedroom.

The sparklers in his head had mixed with the throbbing. He heard more crunching sounds going on up there somewhere. His thoughts were cloudy and muddled, but when he imagined what Reagan had done to Momma, he barely felt the tingling in his lower limbs.

This time, he'd turn the tables for good. Reagan had to be taught a lesson. That bastard would never hurt Momma again.

***

Just as Bobbie reached the doorway, the big man tripped again.

His massive shoulders bumping into the doorframe, he fell heavily to his knees. As he pitched forward, his huge, blood-soaked hand reached out, grasping her left ankle, and pulling her down.

Bobbie twisted to her left and lunged for the railing. She tried to scream, but something prevented her from doing so. A giant wet lump filled her throat.

The huge hand grasping her ankle gave it a sharp twist. A thundering bolt of white-hot pain splashed up her leg, driving a muffled gasp from her throat. She suddenly remembered that this was the same ankle the bastard had grabbed in the truck to haul her out.

She tried once again to grasp the rail, but he yanked her away and twisted her ankle again.

The pain had now become a white-red flash going off, not merely in her leg but all over, up the length of her spine. She feared that if he persisted, her ankle would break like a dead twig.

201

Five feet away, the mortally wounded boy had grunted into a standing position and stumbled over. His jeans and tee shirt were soaked with blood. His tennis shoes looked like they'd been dipped in red paint and squished with every step.

As he limped past, he shouted, in a little boy's voice: "Leave Momma alone, you bastard!" Then he collapsed, dropping to his knees. With a weak cry, he reached out and wrapped his arms around his friend's midsection.

The big man let go of Bobbie's ankle as the boy's weight pushed him down. His struggle was brief; the boy's tremendous grip made him lose his balance.

The two rolled toward the stairs.

His arms and legs wrapped tightly around his friend's torso, the boy hung on. Roaring one last time, the big man reached behind his back, but lacked the strength necessary to pull the boy away. Blood continued flowing from his eye socket.

The boy cried softly, mumbling, "No more games…no more hurt…"

Seconds later, the two went over the top step and rolled down the staircase, one agonizing step at a time, in a disfigured duet of horrifying screams. They broke apart at the bottom of the staircase and lay beside one another, both staring up at the ceiling.

A deafening silence followed.

Shaking violently, Bobbie propped herself up against the banister and gripped the faded wood. Her gaze stayed fixed on the two motionless figures on the floor below. She knew they weren't dead,

202

that they'd get back up in just a couple of seconds and come after her again.

They didn't move.

She waited another minute...and five more minutes. They still didn't move.

When another five peaceful minutes passed, she convinced herself she might have been wrong...that they were both dead. She began to sob, but the sobs were muffled. She noticed only then that the rag was still crammed in her mouth. Groaning, she clawed at the infernal tape covering her lips. Her fingers weren't working right, and she lacked the focus necessary to peel the tape away. To make matters worse, she couldn't steady herself as she worked.

She took a deep breath and fought the approaching dizziness. Both hands came up in a final attempt, her chipped, broken nails digging into the corners of the tape. They sliced into her tender flesh, but she ignored the pain, keeping up the pressure until the square corners of adhesive finally peeled away.

She tossed it over the banister, then lowered her head, opened her mouth and let the soaked rag drop to the floor.

Her gaze returned to the motionless bodies lying at the foot of the staircase. Tears welled in her eyes. With a sigh, she straightened, gripped the banister, lifted her face, and screamed. It felt good—*so* good, in fact, that she decided another one would really hit the spot. But then she realized she had no strength left. She sighed and let her arms drop. Then she fell to the floor.

Sobbing again, she reached out for the railing, closed her eyes and let go of it—and everything else. She didn't even feel the hard wooden floor that came up to whack her on the side of the head.

PART THREE

SURVIVOR

Chapter 34 - 7:30 A.M.

When Bobbie opened her eyes and scanned her surroundings, it took her a while to realize she was lying in a hospital bed.

The whiteness of the walls, the sheets, and the uniforms passing by hurt her eyes. She forced them shut and lay quite still, waiting for her heart to stop pounding. Suddenly afraid, she twisted around painfully and peered between the aluminum rails, expecting to see the big brute and the boy lying on the floor.

There was nothing but shiny linoleum. And there shouldn't be, should there? This wasn't the farmhouse; it was a hospital room, and if there were bodies lying around, they'd be in other beds in other rooms.

Somewhat relieved, she lay back and stared at the white ceiling. Moments later, when her mind cleared, the realization came back, this time much more forcefully. *A hospital room. They found me and brought me here. This means I'm no longer in danger…*

I've survived!

The nightmare came back in cold, dark trickles, and she felt the panic returning. She gazed down at the sheet covering her. A bloody eyeball rested on the sheet between her legs, gawking at her.

My God… She forced her eyes shut, telling herself she was hallucinating, that what she'd just seen was not there. The nightmare was over. The two of them were dead, and she was still alive.

And there was no bloody eyeball lying on her bed.

You're alive, girl. You survived. Open those big brown eyes and start living again…

When she gathered up the strength to open them again, the eyeball was gone.

She lay back and gazed at the ceiling again. There were just too many things to think about, too many things to frighten her and make her heart thump wildly again. It was entirely too much to worry about right now, so she closed her eyes and tried once again to relax.

Before she realized it, she'd fallen asleep.

***

Later, a doctor and a nurse came in and told her about her sprained ankle, bruised ribs, dislocated shoulder, and wrenched spine, and the various bruises and cuts she'd gotten during her bumpy ride to the farmhouse in the back of the farmer's pickup.

She knew all about her injuries but let them ramble on anyway. She didn't want to argue with anyone. She just wanted to rest.

Before they left, they told her the local police wanted to talk to her when she was feeling better.

"Tell them they can talk with me as soon as they like," she said.

The doctor, a tall, slender man in his mid-fifties, acted surprised. "But you need a day or so to recover, to—"

"The sooner, the better." She wanted to get this over with. She hated hospitals, for one thing, and knew that as long as she lay here, thinking about what had happened, the nightmare would stay with her.

The doctor nodded and smiled briefly. Bobbie had the feeling that he somehow understood what she'd just told him. Without another word, he and the nurse left the room.

***

An hour later, two large men in uniforms came in to see her.

The nametag on the shorter and older of the two said Milton, while his partner's tag said Kaminski. She told herself it didn't matter. The only thing that did matter was getting out of here and getting on with her life.

They told her that someone had found the dead farmer, which started the investigation. When the two were found at the bottom of the staircase in the farmhouse, fingerprints were pulled, and the big man was identified by the FBI as a former inmate at the Moundsville prison. Apparently the man had been released early and had been out the last five or six years.

"Then...he *was* from the penitentiary?" She was surprised that her first instinct had been right on the mark.

"Yes, Ma'am," Milton said. "He'd done time for racketeering and other minor stuff. The FBI had

207

their suspicions that he'd been involved in contract murder once or twice before but couldn't seem to put anything together. He always seemed to be one or two steps ahead of the game."

"Too much money restin' on this…"

The brute's startling phrase came right back. This time, however, its message was even more frightening. He was a criminal and had done this at least once or twice before. He was a paid killer and was going to torture and rape her before killing her. Who would want such a horrible thing to happen to her or anyone else? Who would hate Craig so much that they'd pay such a vicious monster to kill him?

And why me? Because I was there? Because I was in the way? Because I'd seen their faces?

Or was it because of something else?

"Ms. Marsh?" Milton was staring. "You all right?"

"I'm just wondering why this all happened," she said absent-mindedly.

"So are we." Kaminski sounded disgusted. "We have our suspicions, but nothing we can put a handle on. If the FBI couldn't nail him using their resources…" He just shrugged.

"How about the boy? He didn't seem much older than eighteen."

"The boy was local. He didn't have a record, so we think he might've just come into the picture by accident."

She was beginning to think that whoever had paid for this to happen was going to get away with it. "Then you really have no idea why this happened?"

They both shook their heads.

"Any ideas?" Milton was staring at her.

She couldn't imagine why anyone would want her dead. She hadn't hurt or betrayed anyone. It wasn't her fault that Craig wanted to have an affair with her. Men had been attracted to her most of her adult life. All she'd done was gone to the farmhouse with Craig; it wasn't as if she'd stabbed Colleen or anyone else in the back in doing so…

What frightened her most of all was that she was still alive, and if she had truly been one of the victims in this murder-for-hire scheme, her life would still be in jeopardy.

But what could she do? How could she prove this? She'd heard the brute say it, but that didn't necessarily mean she could prove it. The man was dead, and unless the police had solid proof of any of this, it would be her word against the anonymous ghoul that had ordered this. And everyone knew what would happen if she cried wolf and the papers got wind of it.

But what if she *didn't* cry wolf? What if she gave everyone the impression that she had no idea what happened? Would the contract still be valid? Or would Craig's murder suffice?

If someone paid that big brute to kill both of them, and if only one of them was actually killed, would the murder contract be satisfied—especially if the killer had died in the process? Or would the person wanting them both dead simply find another killer to finish the contract?

She had one of two choices. She could tell them what she knew and pray that whoever had ordered

Craig dead would be satisfied of the outcome and slither quietly away, without worrying about a massive Federal investigation coming their way...

Or she could keep her mouth shut and hope that whoever had ordered Craig dead had not wanted her dead, too.

"Ms. Marsh?" Milton was waiting.

"I...have no idea," she managed, and hoped she hadn't just signed her own death warrant.

The two men nodded.

"We need to ask you a delicate question," Milton said a moment later. "We don't want to, but we have to. To cover all the bases, we've got to—"

"I understand," she said. "Go ahead and ask."

Kaminski tilted his head. "Were you romantically involved with Mr. Sheffield?"

"He wanted to cheat on his wife with me, but I have a conscience. Marriage has always meant something to me, and I'd never knowingly come between a married couple or even just two people going together. All I did was go with him to see his new investment property. I didn't want to go in the first place, but he lied to me by telling me he wanted my opinion of the place."

Kaminski seemed interested. "He didn't really want your opinion of the place?"

"Actually, he wanted my opinion of the bedroom."

They both nodded, but neither replied.

She was growing tired and found it difficult to keep her eyes open. She didn't care that Kaminski was in the process of asking her another question.

She just closed her eyes and surrendered to the awaiting darkness.

***

Two days later, she was finally allowed to leave the hospital.

She took a cab to the Sheffwares parking garage on Main and 10th Street, where she'd left her two-year-old black Camaro so many eternities ago. She then drove back to her apartment on Main and Market Street. Once it finally registered that she'd come home and that it wasn't just a dream, she found the tension inside her finally beginning to dissolve. She began to relax, and as she stood in the center of her living room, staring in amazement at her personal things, which she once thought she'd never see again, she felt the warm tears of joy drifting down her cheeks.

She spent the rest of the day enjoying her surroundings and watching her favorite movies from her small DVD collection. When she decided to check her voicemail, she discovered seven messages, all from Sheffwares. The phone rang three times that afternoon, but she let it go to voicemail. She didn't want to talk to anyone—especially anyone from the office. Today was to be enjoyed…to be savored…and any contact with the past could simply wait.

***

The next morning, she took a long shower, dried her hair, and pulled on a pair of boot-cut designer jeans, which slipped easily over her bandaged ankle.

211

She put on a pair of comfortable tennis shoes, lacing one of them loosely, again to accommodate her injured ankle. After squirming into one of her favorite tee shirts, the dark-blue one with the white stars forming a brilliant swirl across the front, she got in her Camaro and made the short fifteen-minute trip to the Sheffwares offices. It was painful, walking through those doors and seeing the same faces she'd worked with an eternity ago, but she forced herself down the long hall, past the endless sea of cubicles that had been her world before it had almost been snatched away. She said nothing to anyone, just smiled politely as she limped her way to her cube to clean out her desk.

No more of this company or these people. I need to breathe...to begin living again...

They stopped talking as she drew near, but that didn't bother her. She knew how people were and could only imagine what everyone was told. The story had been on the local news and had hit all the Wheeling and Pittsburgh papers. Most of these folks had no doubt chosen to fill in the details to satisfy their own individual fantasies. She hadn't made any friends since she'd first come on board. However, she'd grown accustomed to this type of treatment. Men always looked at her as some sort of prize or conquest, while women considered her a major threat. And whenever the boss began showing interest, she immediately became hands-off to everyone and was quietly shunned.

But none of that mattered now. All she wanted was to clean out her stuff, stop at the Payroll Office on her way out and make arrangements for her final check to be deposited into her checking account. Then Sheffwares—and all those connected to it— could slip silently into her past with the rest of her bad memories.

It surprised her to discover that it only took her five minutes to fill her tote bag with all her personal stuff. Apparently she hadn't wanted much of herself lingering in this workplace when she'd first started working here. At first she wondered why, then told herself that didn't matter, either. She could think about that once she went back to her apartment to consider her future.

Her phone buzzed the moment she turned away from her desk. It was Craig's partner, Jerry Van Dusen, and he said he needed to talk to her before she left.

Her heart skipped a beat. Of all the people in the company, she disliked Van Dusen the most. He dressed well and looked like he'd just stepped from the glossy color pages of GQ Magazine, but the way he looked at her made her flesh crawl.

"I've just cleaned out my desk, and I'm ready to leave." She tried keeping her voice as pleasant as possible but couldn't keep her contempt for the man bringing out fresh anger she hadn't anticipated.

"We really need to talk, Ms. Marsh."

"But—"

"This won't take five minutes."

She could tell by his tone that she didn't have much of a choice. But if it only meant delaying her freedom another five minutes, what did it matter?

***

213

Jerry Van Dusen sat back in his chair and thought about what he would say to Bobbie Marsh.

The most important thing, of course, was finding out exactly what she knew. All he had to do was ask her a few essential questions. If she knew what really happened out there, he was going to have to make another call to Columbus.

Craig's demise had been coming for a while. It escalated six months ago, when he began acting like a silly high school kid the moment Bobbie Marsh walked into the Sheffwares offices to begin her new job. Craig took one look at the raven-haired beauty and immediately lost all focus. It was as if his brain had instantly switched to sleep mode, and he lost the tough, competitive edge that had enabled him to succeed in software over the last fifteen years.

The Richbourg-Doss-Kennedy deal had been in the works for some time. When Sheffwares stock spiked nearly a year ago, Craig was urged by the Board of Directors, as well as its principal investors, to merge with the Columbus-based conglomerate to get their foot in the door. At that time, the net worth of the corporate real estate giant had exceeded twenty billion and was steadily climbing. Jerry and several other Board members of Sheffwares presented the idea to Craig two months later. To their dismay, Craig hadn't exactly been eager about the idea and had told Alan Richbourg that he needed time to consider the deal.

Several weeks went by, and Craig still hadn't made a decision. When the subject of the merger was brought up again at the quarterly Board meeting, Craig said he needed more time to think about it. Jerry and several of the other board members called an emergency meeting to discuss the matter. They were all in agreement: Craig was either going through a rough patch with Colleen or just didn't like the idea of the merger.

It was later discovered that Craig had withdrawn two million dollars from their corporate account to buy several sections of overgrown weeds near Finley. It was then that the Board decided Craig would have to be confronted about the matter.

The confrontation took place after hours the next day in Craig's office. When he was asked about the Finley property deal, Craig said that he wanted a parcel for a golf course and possibly a bed-and-breakfast-type business to go with it. When Craig was asked why he hadn't told anyone about the deal, he explained that he'd seen the place on the auction block, sensed terrific investment potential and didn't want anyone else to grab it. When he was asked why the company hadn't been told about the withdrawal, he said he'd needed to make a quick decision. And when he was asked why he hadn't made any decision concerning the Richbourg-Doss-Kennedy merger, he merely said that he didn't think it was a good idea.

The Board then knew the entire story. Craig may have bought the property for a couple of commercial projects, but once Bobbie Marsh started working for Sheffwares, it was obvious that he intended to use the existing farmhouse as something slightly more than just a bed-and-breakfast-type venture.

215

The repercussions of such irresponsible decisions would eventually collapse Sheffwares. Craig's wife Colleen would certainly drain the company dry if she discovered what her husband had done with two million dollars of the company's cash reserves. As a major investor of Sheffwares, she could destroy Sheffwares if she withdrew her twenty-five percent share, which translated into holdings totaling fifty-two million. Such an action would not only cause a gaping wound, but it would also disrupt the merger and cause Richbourg-Doss-Kennedy to take their billions elsewhere. Besides Colleen's holdings, nearly forty percent of Sheffwares was owned by Jerry and two other silent partners. If the Richbourg-Doss-Kennedy deal went sour, the company might surely collapse.

A desperate call was made to Richbourg-Doss-Kennedy Corporate Offices in Columbus to arrange an emergency meeting. That same afternoon, one of the conglomerate's representatives flew by charter to Wheeling. The rep listened to the problem and told them the matter would be taken care of. One of Richbourg-Doss-Kennedy's more influential contacts might be interested in purchasing several sections of uncleared farmland in the Ohio Valley area. Certain extreme arrangements could be made to obtain the parcel for commercial purposes.

Sheffwares was contacted the next day and given the news that Richbourg-Doss-Kennedy was in the process of acquiring a six-hundred-plus-acre section of prime farmland that would be developed into a series of condominiums, a strip mall and a golf course. The two-year project was estimated at two hundred and fifty million dollars.

Once everything was in place, the only thing to be done was to deal with the original buyer of the investment property.

Jerry sat back and rubbed his eyes. The contract had somehow messed up, but the end result had taken place satisfactorily. Craig had been his good friend and close business partner the last fifteen years. However, business was business, and Craig had nearly ruined everything over a few radical ideas and a piece of tail he could get anywhere in Wheeling for a couple of hundred bucks.

Now, as he sat at his desk, waiting tensely for her to come in, he realized what might have to be done. If Bobbie Marsh gave any indication that she was aware of a murder contract and that Sheffwares was even remotely involved, she'd have to be eliminated.

It was that simple.

***

He was standing behind his desk when she went in.

He was tall, distinguished and impeccably dressed, his red hair professionally styled to make him look boyish, even though he was just a year or two shy of forty. Like all his suits, this one looked custom-fitted and probably came from Italy. She couldn't see his shoes but guessed they were also imported from Italy. To the casual observer, Jerry Van Dusen displayed the picture of extraordinary success and ultimate perfection. To her, he would always be something that had crawled out from underneath a rock.

"Have a seat."

She didn't want to drag this out, so she limped over to the chair and sat.

He sat down and gazed at her for nearly half a minute. She stared right back, and for the first time realized that she no longer felt any hatred or disgust. She felt only pity, because she knew that in spite of the fact that he was fabulously wealthy and successful, he couldn't have everything he wanted. He couldn't because he could never have her.

"I hope your ankle's mending satisfactorily."

"I'm doing all right."

He gestured to her face, where the three tiny bandages covered the cuts she'd made from her nails ripping off the tape. "How about—"

"They're just superficial."

He nodded. "I guess you know by now that what happened to you and Craig has been all over the news."

She didn't reply. She suspected he was after something, so she decided to let him talk.

"When I first heard, I made dozens of phone calls, of course. I was determined to get to the truth as quickly as possible. I understand—that is, I was told by the local police—that you and Craig were assaulted by two criminals while Craig was showing you his new real estate investment."

Again, she said nothing.

"I understand the local police talked to you at the hospital."

She nodded.

218

"Could you tell me what they told you?"

"Such as?"

"Anything about the killers?"

"They told me they don't know much."

"How much *do* they know?"

She blinked. Her suspicions grew. Some strong inner sense told her to tell him as little as possible. For some reason, he seemed to be pumping her for information. She began to wonder if he knew more about what happened than he was letting on. "They told me one of them had served time in Moundsville, and that the other had no record."

"I was told the same thing." He consulted his watch—that imported Patek Philippe Nautilus 40MM Rose Gold timepiece he was forever showing people and bragging that it cost him more than ninety thousand dollars. He obviously considered it a symbol of success. Bobbie considered it a symbol of his colossal phoniness.

"Is that why you wanted me here?" she asked. "To ask me things I obviously know nothing about?"

"I wanted to ask you what Craig told you before…well, before he—"

"Before he was murdered?" A wave of anger sliced through her. This man couldn't even say the word. "Is that what you mean?"

He didn't reply right off. She could tell that what she'd said bothered him. It made her feel a little better.

"I guess I'm just wondering about his intentions—with the property, of course. It *is* a sizeable investment, and since he didn't discuss it with me or the Board, or put it in his will—"

"He wanted to make it into a golf course. And maybe a bed-and breakfast setup for the farmhouse."

Van Dusen nodded. "What else did he tell you?"

She sighed. "About what?"

He just stared at her.

Bobbie couldn't help feeling more suspicion flaring up. Why was he so interested? More importantly, why wasn't he more broken up about Craig's murder? He and Craig had been friends for years—he just wasn't nearly as torn up as he should be. Wouldn't he be asking questions about what happened, rather than inquiring about Craig's investment, or what the local police had told her?

She decided to stir him up a little more. "Did they tell you how Craig died?" she asked.

"They…didn't go into details."

"Would you like to know?"

After a considerable pause, he said, "I really don't think it's relevant how—"

"He choked on his own vomit."

The man paled instantly.

"The two who came after us tied him up and taped his mouth shut. Then they carried him inside and tossed him on the bed. Later on, Craig threw up, and—"

"I get it."

Bobbie wanted to tell him more of what she saw. She strongly suspected that Van Dusen didn't want to know the details. This feeling made the wave of anger come back, but she took a breath and forced it away.

It took him a few moments to collect himself. Then he said, "I'm wondering if you think the two who did this chose Craig's farmhouse at random."

"Random?"

He shrugged. "I'm just thinking out loud, I guess."

"What else could have happened?"

"I honestly don't know."

He leaned forward and gazed into her eyes. "You really and truly have no idea why this happened?"

She saw something in his eyes she hadn't noticed before. It was fear. The man was afraid of something.

But why was he afraid? Did he dread the publicity? The embarrassment of the company? A drop in Sheffwares stock? What could have him so spooked that he'd—

No. It couldn't be.

"Too much money restin' on this…"

Her suspicions hit the roof.

Was Jerry Van Dusen involved in this? Was this his scheme? His contract? What if *he* was the one who'd arranged this? What if *he* was the one responsible for those two coming out to the farmhouse?

What if this bastard, who'd been a close friend of Craig's for more than a decade, wanted them both dead? What if Craig had done something he shouldn't have done and had angered the wrong people?

221

And now his good friend wanted to know what she knew.

Be very, very careful, her inner voice told her. *If this man really did arrange to have you and Craig murdered, he's not going to stand idly by if he thinks you suspect him or know what was going on.*

Her entire body suddenly felt as though it had been submerged in hot water. It took her considerable control to keep from trembling. *Keep it inside. You may have killed the two murderers and escaped slow, agonizing death in the process, but you're facing it once again, and if you say the wrong thing…*

He couldn't know. Even if she was one hundred percent totally wrong, Jerry Van Dusen *must not know* what she thought—or even suspected—about all this.

"I think the cops were right," she said, surprised that her voice sounded so calm. "I think those two committed a crime somewhere in Wheeling, Shadyside or Bridgeport and were looking for a place to hole up. The farmhouse was isolated. It would have been perfect for what they were looking for."

The fear in Van Dusen's eyes vanished and was replaced with relief. Just then, he sat back. And smiled. "That's what I think, too, as a matter of fact."

She knew right then that she didn't want to stay in this room any longer. The anger and the disgust were making her nauseous, and she realized that if she stayed one minute longer, she'd give herself

222

away. Mindful of her ankle, she got up. "I really need to go—"

"I called you in here for another reason," he said rather quickly.

She stared at him and waited.

"I called you in to ask if you'd consider signing a waiver."

"What kind of waiver?"

"We all realize what you've been through, but we'd also like you to consider the company's position in this rather delicate matter. I'm sure you realize that Sheffwares had absolutely nothing to do with what happened, and that—"

"You'd like me to sign something that says I won't sue Sheffwares for what I just went through?"

After a moment, he gave a slight nod.

As she stared at his sparkling, impeccably clean-shaven face, she realized just how nauseous the man made her. She was more than convinced at that moment that her suspicions had been right on. She'd read about corporate corruption…about secret deals…and payoffs…and hush money…and getting troublesome people out of the way. It happened everywhere.

The thought of it made her want to throw up.

But now she knew she had to keep the memories—and the terror—buried deep inside her. She knew she could do it because she'd become quite good at holding things in. She'd spent most of her short life holding in her feelings, her emotions. She'd become expert at keeping things to herself, things that would hurt certain people if she let them out.

After all, she'd hidden from two killers and had done a damned fine job of it. She'd kept her horror hidden, as well as her inner torment and her fears. And she could keep her anger and outrage hidden as well.

You've got to take your hatred, anger, outrage, and suspicions and lock them away. If you give this impeccably dressed monster even the slightest hint that you suspect him for this, you know what he'll do, because if you're right, you already know what he's capable of.

"Well?" He was waiting. "Will you sign the waiver?"

"Of course," she said.

Van Dusen didn't really *smile*, but she could tell he wanted to. "Sheffwares thanks you, Miss Marsh."

She bent over and signed the paper he pushed in her direction.

As she signed, he said, "We'd also like to give you a fifty-thousand-dollar severance check as a token of our gratitude—and, of course, for your troubles."

She stopped writing and met his eyes. "Did you just say…fifty thousand dollars?"

He shrugged. "You've just been through a horrible ordeal. Please let us try and recompense you in some way. It's the least we can do."

It was hush money. Anyone could figure that one out. But even though the idea of accepting money for this disgusted her beyond words, she knew better than refuse.

"Well? Will you let us try and recompense you for all this?"

Hold it in... Keep it in there even if you think you'll burst wide open...

"Yes. Of course."

The bastard sighed in relief.

She forced out one last smile then limped as quickly as she could out of his office. As she stepped outside into the early afternoon sunlight, she couldn't believe how clear the day looked. The foul city smells that had disgusted her so much in the past were gone, and the gray clouds normally hovering above the town appeared lighter and wispier beneath a flawless blue sky.

Was this bright new day telling her in its own subtle way that the new chapter in her life would be different? She'd heard and read things about people who'd faced violent death and survived. They all said the same thing—that the following day looked cleaner, the air smelled fresher, and the clouds resembled the feathers of doves.

One thing at a time, she told herself. And as she faced this new chapter in her life, she felt that as long as she kept the bad stuff hidden and buried, she just might be able to begin her immediate future on a fresh, positive note.

OTHER WORKS BY DAVID BERARDELLI

THE APPRENTICE
THE WAGON DRIVER
DEMONCHASER
DEMONCHASER II
STEPPING OUT OF MY GRAVE
ESCAPE CLAUSE
FATAL INNOCENCE
THE FUNNY DETECTIVE
JUST A SIMPLE ERRAND
COLORS
WORKING FOR A MOB BOSS
AND DARKNESS FELL
AFTER DARKNESS FELL
DEMONCHASER III
IN ANOTHER REALM
BEYOND RECOGNITION
LOOKING FOR A DEAD GUY
THE NIGHTMARE COLLECTOR
HUNTING THE TALL BLONDE
ENLIGHTENMENT
REDEMPTION
A RIPPLE IN TIME
YESTERDAY'S JOURNEY
WINTER SCENE
THE PLANNING COMMITTEE

Titles available through:
Fiction4All
https://fiction4all.com